C000271582

By the same author:

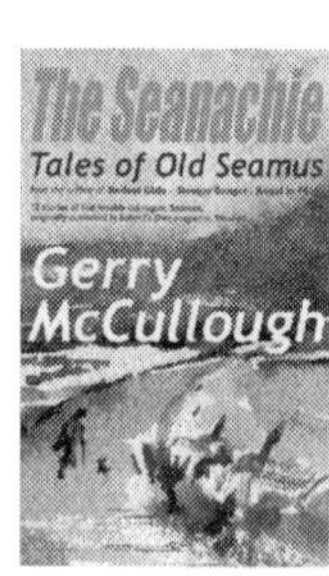

Cover design: Raymond McCullough

Cover painting: Ken Riddles, Bangor, NI

The Seanachie 4

Paddy and the Snake

... and other stories

Gerry McCullough

Published by

ISBN 13: 978-0 9955404 4 6

ISBN 10: 0-9955404 4 6

First published **2019**

10a Listooder Road, Crossgar,

Downpatrick, Northern Ireland BT30 9JE

Contents

Thanks to my husband, Raymond, for cover design, editing, proof-reading and general encouragement.

Introduction

The first story I ever had published was *A Tale of a Teacup*, in the all Ireland magazine, *Ireland's Own*. This was the first Old Seamus story, and it's included in my earlier collection, *The Seanachie: Tales of Old Seamus*. Because of this I have a very soft spot in my heart for it, and for all my Old Seamus stories. I've written 72 of them by now, and will go on writing them as long as my editor wants me to, and as long as the ideas keep coming.

I love the setting and the atmosphere. Whenever I start a Tale of Old Seamus, it's as if I've been transported not only to the Irish county of Donegal but to the days of long ago when Old Seamus himself was younger and when life was simpler and happier. Donegal is a beautiful place, ideal for a holiday, wild and relaxing.

Above all, I love Old Seamus himself, and his happy-go-lucky attitude to life. Seamus gets by without a nine to five job, and enjoys himself day by day. He makes a living from poaching and by keeping hens and bees. He doesn't allow anyone to order him around or tell him what he should do. He has his own ideas about right and wrong, which mainly focus on helping people in trouble.

My first person narrator, Jamie, is a young man who loves to go up to Donegal, as he often explains, to get away from his busy city job, and to stay in the little white-washed cottage which he inherited from his grandparents, in the fictional Donegal village of Ardnakil.

As a child he often visited his grandparents there, and it was at that time that he first made friends with Seamus O'Hare, that disreputable old rogue, poacher and rascal, who taught Jamie everything he knows about the animals and flowers of the countryside. Seamus is an inveterate storyteller (which is what Seanachie means in Irish), and he loves to sit back, relax, and tell yet another story from his past. Jamie loves to listen – and I hope you will, too!

In this collection there's *'Seamus And The Crafty Beast'* – where Seamus solves the mystery of the disappearing hens and proves a little girl's pet blameless; *'Paddy and the Snake'* – Paddy loves to play practical jokes, but he's not so happy when one rebounds on him! In *'Romance and Father Gillespie'*, a young Seamus discovers a priest's passion, but promises to keep his secret – yet in *'Seamus Takes a Ride'* he threatens to reveal all; and in *'Daisy in the Country'* being an innocent about country matters is all to the good from the point of view of Daisy's boyfriend, Michael!

1 Summer Storm

The sun blazed down from a hot blue summer sky. It was a day to be near running water, indeed a day for being inside a cool, flowing stream. Not too far from the small white-washed cottage, which had been left to me by my grandparents in the little Donegal village of Ardnakil, was a river which answered to that description in all respects. I set off towards it, strolling at my ease, for, after all, I was on my holiday break from my busy city job, relaxing for a few days in this little place I loved. There was no rush.

On all sides there was green grass, trees with fresh new green leaves, banks scattered with coloured flowers, wild and sweet smelling. I drew a deep breath, and rounded a bend in the country lane to see the river stretching before me at its widest point. And there, as I had half expected, was my old friend Seamus O'Hare, thigh deep in the running stream, casting his line skilfully across the smooth, silvery water.

He must have heard my approach, for as he turned his head there was a momentary frown on his wrinkled old brown face. Then the frown disappeared and a beaming smile lit up his eyes. He ran one hand through the curly white hair which matched his luxuriant beard, and cried out, 'Jamie! Great to see you, boy! Sit yourself down on the riverbank for a moment, and don't speak, don't even breathe! I've got something on this line that I don't want to let go of!'

So I sat down on the thick grass, studded with buttercups and creamy clover, lay back chewing a strand, and watched with admiration as Seamus played his fish. Some ten minutes later, a huge silver trout had joined about half a dozen more in his creel, and Seamus climbed out of the river, sat beside me, and took out his disreputable old pipe, which he proceeded to light and puff at with every evidence of enjoyment.

'What a day, boy!' was his first comment.

'Marvellous,' I agreed. 'Do you think the weather will last?'

Seamus cast a knowledgeable look over the sky. 'No way will it last!' he told me. 'There'll be thunder before many hours, or I know nothing about it.'

And since I'd known Seamus since my childhood, and considered him a fount of all knowledge when it came to the countryside – from birds, fish and flowers to the weather – I believed him.

'I think we'd better be strolling along as far as the *Golden Pheasant*, boy,' Seamus said. He cast another look at the sky. 'It'll take us a quarter of an hour or so – I wouldn't want to be out here much longer. I'm selling these fish to the owner, Willie Brennan. But I'd planned to keep one of the smaller ones back for my tea, later. I'll make it two, if you'd like to join me.'

And with my enthusiastic agreement, we packed up and set off in the direction of the village.

Presently we were seated at a table in the window of the *Golden Pheasant* bar, with a pint each in front of us. As we looked out at the bridge across the river running through the middle of Ardnakil, I saw the sky had abruptly darkened. A moment later rain came lashing down in torrents. As I held my breath, the crash of thunder followed fast on a streak of lightening.

'Some storm, Jamie,' Seamus remarked happily. 'We don't get too many in this part of the world, but when they come they're worth watching – if you're safe inside, that is. Did I ever tell you the story of Artie Conlon and the thunderstorm?'

'No, I don't believe you did, Seamus,' I said, leaning back lazily. 'Go ahead and tell me it now.'

'Artie was a nice young fella,' said Seamus, 'the son of some old friends of mine. But he never amounted to much. He would have a decent enough job, and then he would chuck it up for a while and try out some experiment or other – he was convinced that one day he'd make his fortune with an invention that would rock civilisation – and then he'd have to take another job for a while, until he would throw it up, too.

People were inclined to laugh at him, although at the same time nearly everyone liked him, for he was a kind-hearted lad who'd go out of his way to help you. But he wasn't what you'd consider good husband material, and it was no wonder that Eileen Flaherty took no interest in him, and seemed to despise him, more than anything else.

Eileen was a good-looking girl, and could have taken her pick of all the neighbouring boys. But so far she hadn't said yes to any of them. She had a good job in the big draper's shop in Millerstown, so although her parents were both dead, Eileen could support herself, and had no need of a husband unless she really fell for someone.

It was clear to everyone that Artie was mad about her, but whether Eileen herself realised, I didn't know. She showed no sign of interest, at any rate.

Artie had talked to me about her, but I hadn't much in the way of advice to give him. 'She might think better of you if you'd settle to something, Artie,' was all I could think of. 'She's hardly the girl to take on a husband she has to support!'

Artie groaned. 'I hate these indoor jobs, Seamus,' he told me. 'Shops and offices – I can only stand them for so long. But …' – he brightened up – '… I've come up with a great idea for a food that makes animals easy to manage, without harming them in any way. It would be great for bulls and such like …'

'Well, we'll see Artie,' was all I said, for he'd had so many good ideas that had come to nothing that I hadn't much faith in this new one. But as it turned out, I was wrong.

The weather had been just like this week, hot and heavy. Eileen, not being as weather-wise as you might expect from a country girl – after all, she spent most of her time working indoors in the draper's shop – had decided to go for a walk on her afternoon off. She was dandering through the woods, enjoying the shade from the trees and the gold of the sunlight filtering through the green of the leaves. Artie, as he told me afterwards, had noticed her setting off, and was following her at a discreet distance, hoping to catch up with her sort of accidentally on purpose.

Just as it did today, the sky suddenly darkened. Eileen looked up in surprise at the sky. Then, as the first scattered drops of the coming thunder-storm began to fall, she took to her heels and raced through the trees. There was a tumbledown old one-room cottage, she knew, not far off, and she wanted to get there before the rain soaked her new summer frock and ruined her hairdo.

She was a slim young lass, and some sprinter, and sure enough she made it to the cottage in time, pushed the door open and was inside in two shakes of a lamb's tail, before the first bucketfuls came emptying down.

Meanwhile Artie wasn't slow about taking off himself, and though it crossed his mind that Eileen mightn't be too pleased if he joined her in the cottage uninvited, he was more concerned, to tell you the truth, with keeping dry, than with worrying about that.

A few moments later, he had shoved open the door and was charging inside without a second's thought.

He heard a loud gasp, and peered round him. He took it for granted that it was Eileen, reacting to his sudden entrance, but it was so dark that it was a bit hard for Artie to tell who it was or where it was coming from. But a moment later there was another streak of lightening, and he could see Eileen's face lit up, as white as a sheet. He had time to wonder if she was as scared as all that just because he had burst into the cottage unexpectedly, and then suddenly she had hurled herself at him and was in his arms, clinging on for dear life.

'Artie! Artie!' she panted. 'Help! Save me! There's a ghost groaning at the back of the cottage somewhere!'

Artie was torn. It was great to have Eileen nestling in his arms, but a ghost didn't sound so good. He wasn't too sure whether to be bouncing with happiness or terrified. Still, Eileen was solid and real, and the ghost probably wasn't.

'There, there, pet,' he murmured into her hair. 'Artie'll look after you!' He followed up his good fortune by turning her face up towards his own and kissing her quite a lot.

It was some time later when a noise came faintly to his ears.

Groan! Groan!

Artie stiffened. Eileen's opening words, which he had put aside as the sort of thing girls imagined in the dark, came back to him.

'Who – who's there?' he stuttered, and the noise came again.

But Artie was a different man, now that he'd held Eileen Flaherty in his arms, and found that she was kissing him back.

'It's all right, Eileen,' he said, putting her firmly behind his back. 'Don't you be worrying. I'll look after you.'

And with a bold step he made his way towards the back of the cottage, determined not to let Eileen down.

'Come out, ye scoundrel!' he ordered, putting a brave face on it – for he wasn't all that sure there was nothing to worry about. The response nearly made him run for it. An even louder groan came from the back of the room. Then another bolt of lightning lit up the cottage, and Artie saw what it was that was making the noise.

Lying on the floor, moving about in distress, was a large cow – or was it a bull?

Artie couldn't be sure which it was. But one thing was clear to him. This was his opportunity to prove once and for all that his new invention worked. He had something which would, he believed, calm down the fiercest bull. He was determined to try it out now, or die in the attempt.

Fishing in his pocket, he drew out a handful of his new invention and, kneeling down beside the stricken animal, he held it gently to the soft mouth and, speaking soothingly, encouraged him or her to eat.

To his delight, the cow, as he now saw it was – the udders were the clue – began to lap slowly at his palm, taking in the mixture. Presently, the moaning sound ceased, as Artie gently stroked the cow's sides. To his surprise and delight, he saw a delicate, slim-legged calf emerging. The little animal staggered to its feet, stumbled about for a moment, then knelt down by its mother's side and began gratefully to imbibe the cow's sweet milk. Artie felt a thrill of pleasure as he watched it.

Meanwhile Eileen, creeping carefully forward, watched the new-born calf and its mother with an unexpected joy which for a while left her unable to do anything but smile happily.

When she could speak at last, she said, 'Artie, you're wonderful! How clever you are, helping the poor cow to give birth! And what a beautiful little calf!'

Artie wasn't too sure that he deserved her praise – but he didn't say so. Instead, he clasped her masterfully in his arms again, and said, 'Eileen, you're going to marry me! Do you understand?'

And Eileen murmured, 'Yes, Artie, darling. Whatever you say.'

It turned out that the cow belonged to Barney Kennedy, who farmed the land nearby. She had wandered off from the field where Barney had thought she was safe enough, eating the grass and getting ready to give birth to her new calf, and the thunderstorm had driven her into the tumbledown old cottage, where her birth pangs had come on her unexpectedly.

It wasn't so much the invention, the food mixture, which Artie had fed her, as his comfort to her in need, which had helped the cow in her delivery. Farmer Kennedy, hearing the story from the enthusiastic Eileen and the rather more modest Artie, was very grateful. The outcome was that he offered Artie a job on his farm – his cowman had left, which was why the cow had been able to wander astray so easily.

Artie, realising for the first time that a job in the open air on a farm was the ideal one for him, away from shops and offices, accepted eagerly. So now he was in an excellent position to marry Eileen – who, I might add, was only too happy to marry him!

'So that was one storm, at any rate,' said Seamus, 'that brought a happy result! Come on, Jamie. Our own storm's over. Let's go and cook that fish, now!'

2 Seamus and the Crafty Beast

A fine loud cackling noise assaulted my ears as I strolled happily down a country lane which led to the tumbledown cottage, just outside the small Donegal village of Ardnakil, where my friend old Seamus O'Hare lived. It was a fine Spring day, neither too hot nor too cold, with a fresh breeze fluttering the small new leaves on hedge and tree. The sound of bird-song announced that the swallows were beginning to return and set up home, after their winter holiday abroad in warmer climates.

I turned the corner, saw the cottage, and realised that the cackling came from a flock of multi-coloured hens scratching and pecking on the piece of ground which Seamus sometimes jokingly referred to as his front lawn.

One fat brown hen with an upstanding red comb rushed towards me, then backed hurriedly away again as I continued to move forward. The others herded together in a flurried crowd and headed off round the corner of the cottage, making a great noise about it as they went.

I found myself laughing. I wasn't afraid of hens. My grandparents had kept a dozen or so, when I used to visit them, as a child, in the little Ardnakil cottage which I'd since inherited. It was very pleasant to see this bunch running wild again, as they used to do in the days of my childhood, instead of being locked away in factory conditions.

Just then my old friend Seamus came round the corner, his wrinkled brown face alight with smiles and his curly white hair sticking out in all directions under his battered old cap, blown by the Spring breeze.

'Jamie!' he greeted me. 'Great to see you again, boy! Come round the back and have a sit down while I get you something to drink.'

We turned the corner of the cottage into the wilderness of Seamus's back garden, a riot of newly blossoming bluebells, apple blossom, and bushes thick with the buds which promised blackcurrants, gooseberries, and later on blackberries in abundance in their due season, with rows of potato plants and the leaves of future tall peas and beans on their stalks. Amid this profusion the brown, white and speckled hens darted about, pecking among the grass for insects and seeds. Seamus waved me into one of the comfortable chairs he had placed under the eaves of the cottage, sheltered from the breeze.

'Well, Seamus,' I greeted him when he appeared presently with two brimming beer tankards filled with the black stuff, 'this is a new departure for you!'

'The hens? Ah, no, Jamie, I used to keep hens a good while ago. I was given some by old Sarah McFarland, as a sort of thank you for something I'd done for her. But I gave it up when they stopped laying. I just took a notion to try it again, lately. There's nothing to beat a good fresh egg. I'll boil you a couple presently for your tea, if you like.'

'That sounds great, Seamus. But why did Sarah give you the hens in the first place? Sounds to me there might be a story there?'

'Well, and so there is, Jamie. Would you like me to tell you about it?' Seamus settled himself back into his chair, sipped at his tankard, took a pull at his disreputable old pipe and without more ado began.

Old Sarah McFarland was a great one for the hens. She made a living by selling the eggs to a big shop in Millerstown, who sent a van round to collect them fresh from her every morning, and she looked after those hens of hers as if they were children. So when they started disappearing one by one, leaving nothing behind but a trail of blood and feathers, she was rightly upset.

'Something's getting into the hen run at night, Seamus,' she wailed to me when I happened to drop in one day in passing (in the hope of a free egg or two, if the truth be known). 'I don't know what or who it is, but I'll find out, that's for sure!'

I was sorry about her trouble, but there seemed little I could do at the time.

However, a few days later, I heard more about it, this time from a different source.

Young Millie Morrison was a nice little girl that I was friendly with. She wasn't much more than nine or ten at this time, and she was an orphan, living with her auntie Emily O'Hara, a strict, upright woman willing to do her best for Millie, but not always too wise in how she went about it. I came across Millie one day, as she was rushing out of her Auntie Emily's house just as I was passing by. She was roaring at the top of her voice, 'Don't you dare, Auntie Emily! I'll never speak to you again! I'll run away from home! I hope your bees all sting you and your honey goes bad in the comb, it'd serve you right, you cruel pig!'

And she slammed the cottage door loud enough to be heard in Donegal town.

I couldn't help laughing at the mixture of it, but I could see the child was really upset, so I took her by the arm gently and I said, 'Whoa, whoa, Millie! What's all the noise about?'

Then I led her along the lane a bit out of her auntie's sight and hearing.

'Now, Millie,' I said, 'Sit down here on the bank and tell me all about it.' So we sat side by side on the bank with the hawthorn blossom hanging over us and the buttercups growing all round us, and Millie explained.

It seemed that Sarah McFarland had been round to see Millie's Auntie Emily who was a great pal of hers, and had told her about the hens. And between the two of them they'd come up with the idea that the culprit was Millie's cat, Paddy Whiskers.

Millie had had Paddy since he was a kitten. She'd found and adopted him as a stray, and she'd lavished all her love on him for the past two years. He was a fully grown tom by then, but in Millie's eyes he was still the helpless, sweet little kitten she'd found, and she was fiercely protective of him.

'I know Paddy Whiskers would never touch her old hens, Seamus!' she said. The anger was still there not far beneath the surface, and an inclination to burst into tears wasn't much behind it. 'They just think so because they want someone to blame. Sarah McFarland says she's seen him round the hencoop in the evenings, more than once. But he likes to wander about. He's well fed at home, why would he be going after hens?'

'Indeed, it seems unlikely, Millie,' I said.

'Seamus, Auntie Emily says she's going to have him put down! She says she can't have Paddy Whiskers upsetting the neighbours and putting her on bad terms with them! I hate her, I hate her! Oh Seamus, can't you do something to stop her?'

'Now, Millie, you'd need to calm down, pet, and you mustn't say you hate your Auntie Emily. She's only trying to do what she thinks is right. But –' I held up a finger to prevent a further outburst – 'it may be that there's something I can do to help. I'll start by having a word with her, to make sure she holds her fire and doesn't do anything drastic about Paddy just yet.'

Millie turned a beaming face up to me. 'Oh, Seamus, if you can do that, I'll love you forever!' she said fervently.

I made a point of calling with Miss Emily O'Hara that same afternoon, and I let her know that I thought Paddy Whiskers wasn't the culprit, and I got her to promise that she wouldn't do anything until at least the next day.

Then I went round to see old Sarah McFarland.

'Ye see, Sarah,' I said at the end of some earnest conversation, 'I'm out in the woods sometimes at night, and what I've seen lately may well be the solution of the mystery. I may be able to put my finger on the thief who's been stealing your hens. I'll make a point of looking out for him tonight, and then you'll know where you are.'

Sarah was bubbling over with gratitude by the time I left. 'I'd just like to know the truth, Seamus,' she said. 'Heaven knows I don't want to blame the child's cat if it's not him that's been doing it.'

I lay out in the woods near Sarah's cottage that night. It was a full moon, and almost as bright as daylight. It wasn't one of my usual haunts, for all I'd told Sarah, for there were no pheasants to be had there. But in spite of that, there aren't any woods or fields round Ardnakil, or even much further afield, that I don't know well.

I hadn't been there an hour when I saw the gleam of something green, coming stealthily across the clearing beside me. It was a pair of bright, beautiful eyes. A moment later, I could make out the shape. Just as I thought, it was a fox. A vixen, if I was any judge, on the hunt to provide for her den full of newly born cubs.

I wished her well in her hunt. But I couldn't allow her to continue to rob Sarah McFarland of her hens and her livelihood, let alone cause the death of young Millie's pet.

The fox moved stealthily on, and I allowed her to get a reasonable distance before I slid cautiously out of my hiding place among the low undergrowth and followed silently after her.

Sure enough, she was headed for the hen run beside Sarah's cottage.

The hens were safely inside the coop for the night, roosting in what they thought was safety. I wondered how the vixen was managing to get in. That was one of the main things I was there to find out. I'd seen the fox several nights ago, but hadn't, at that time, thought it was any of my business to follow her and find out where her hunt was taking her. Now it was a different matter.

Sarah had a fence around her property, a sturdy looking construction which she was relying on to keep out intruders of any kind, human or animal. I watched from a safe distance as Mistress Fox made her way without hesitation to one particular place. This was evidently a familiar proceeding.

A moment later, I saw that she had disappeared through a loose plank, emerging inside the run. The door of the coop wasn't locked. A nudge of the vixen's head pushed it open. It was time for me to act.

I sprang to my feet, hollered at the top of my voice, 'Sarah! Come here! Robbery!' and watched with satisfaction as the thief fled from the door of the coop, wriggled back through the fence, and with a bound was back in the cover of the woods, heading for home and safety. It was no part of my plan that she should be caught.

I watched as the lights went up in Sarah's cottage, and a few minutes later the lady herself came rushing out, a shawl flung hurriedly over her thick nightgown and her white hair standing on end.

'What is it, Seamus? What is it?' she called.

'A fox, Sarah!' I told her. 'I had my suspicions – I saw her in the woods a few nights ago. But I didn't know about your hens until today. There's your culprit!'

'Can we catch her, Seamus?' Sarah howled furiously, but I calmed her down.

'No, Sarah – she's safe away. But you can see the evidence – look, there's her tracks.' The bright moonlight showed clearly the imprints of the vixen's feet. Sarah looked and was convinced.

'And, Sarah,' I went on, 'if you get someone to mend your fence' – I pointed out the loose plank – 'and get them to check for any other weaknesses at the same time, and if you put a lock on the door of your coop, and fasten it at nights, your problems will be over. You'll need to get up and let the hens out in the morning, mind you. I know it's a nuisance, but better than losing a hen every night, isn't it?'

Sarah was all over me. She couldn't say enough to thank me. And it was the same with young Millie the next day, when Sarah went round to apologise to Emily O'Hara and assure them that poor Paddy Whiskers had been falsely accused. Millie's beaming face was reward enough for me.

But I didn't object, mind you, when Sarah gave me half a dozen of her best hens! For years I enjoyed the fresh eggs on a regular basis, until the hens got past it.

I remembered the story recently, and I thought I'd give the hen keeping another go. Would you fancy a couple of lovely fresh boiled eggs now, Jamie? I'll go and put some on!

3 Queen of the Bees

Summer was still with us. I could feel the hot rays beating down on my back as I strolled in a leisurely fashion through the country lanes near my little whitewashed cottage in the small Donegal village of Ardnakil. I was on a break from my demanding city job, doing nothing in particular for a change and thoroughly enjoying it. I could smell the honeysuckle in the hedges as I passed by and when presently I branched off to cross an open field there were daisies, clover and forget-me-nots growing underfoot among the grass.

I wondered if my old friend Seamus O'Hare was about. I might call at his tumbledown old cottage. It wasn't far away. It was hard to believe Seamus would be indoors on what he would call, 'Such a grand day.' Still, I turned aside on the spur of the moment and a few minutes later was pushing open the rickety old gate to what Seamus calls his garden – a wilderness of beauty.

The air was heavy with the scents of the mixed wild flowers growing in profusion, and I could hear a gentle murmur which I presently identified as the humming of many bees. I made my way round the corner of the cottage and there I tracked the buzzing to its source. Along the high hedge of escallonia which ran on one side of the back garden grew a mass of pink blossoms, and on every blossom there was a large, fat, black and yellow striped bee, industriously sucking up the nectar to make honey.

Seamus was over in the far corner, bending over a couple of bee hives, his face masked by a veil of netting and his hands covered and protected by thick gardening gloves.

'This is a new one to me, Seamus!' I greeted him. 'So you're a beekeeper now, are you?'

'Ah, well, Jamie,' replied my old friend, pushing up his veil to show the merry twinkling eyes in his wrinkled brown face, and beaming happily, 'with the shortage of bees we've been having for the past few years, I thought I'd try my hand at it, and see if I could help to bring up the numbers a bit.'

'Good idea, Seamus!'

'And then, it's always nice to get the honey, as well, see.' Seamus stopped whatever he was doing and peeled off his gloves. 'Come and sit down for a while, Jamie, and I'll get us both a cool drink.'

He led the way to a couple of rickety garden chairs, produced a jug of homemade lemonade, and said, 'Mind you, I used to keep bees a long while ago. Not that I was the best at it, now. Or so my friend Peggy Coyle used to tell me. But, sure, according to Peggy, there was no one any good at the bee keeping bar herself. Until the day she came up across Sean McGilligan, that is.'

'Tell me about it, Seamus,' I invited him. I lay back lazily in perfect contentment, sipped my lemonade and prepared to listen.

Peggy Coyle was a bright, cheerful soul. Left an orphan at an early age, she'd been supporting herself by the sale of eggs and vegetables for a few years before she took to the bee keeping. But once started on that, there was no looking back for Peggy. She boasted that her honey was the best for miles around, and sure most people would have agreed with her. She took a stall at the market at Millerstown every weekend, and sold her week's product there with no problem.

Then came the day when a rival bee keeper, and honey producer, set up on a stall not far from Peggy's own. In fact, it was so close that anyone coming to Peggy's stall was bound to see it. This was Sean McGilligan, and, crafty man that he was, he sold his honey for just a bit less per pot than Peggy, so that when the people coming to buy from her saw his prices, it wasn't a bit of wonder that they took to turning aside and buying from Sean instead. What's more, Sean was a loud, friendly man, full of jokes and laughter, so that he attracted folks to his stall even apart from his low prices. It was a pleasure to buy from him, or so many a person told me.

Sean came from Ardnakil, but a long time ago he'd taken himself off to America to make his fortune. Whether or not he'd made it I never heard, but now he'd come back home with enough money to buy a small sort of a farm just outside the village, with enough ground to support himself in potatoes and vegetables and to keep a large number of bees. And here he was at the market every week, undercutting Peggy.

Peggy tried reducing her own price, but sure, no sooner did Sean see her charging less that himself than he cut his own price again, so that before many weeks were past, poor Peggy found that she was making less and less every time she went to market.

She came to see me in despair.

'What am I to do, Seamus?' she asked me. 'If this goes on I'll soon be poorer than a church mouse, without a penny to scratch myself with!'

I was right and sorry for Peggy, but just then I didn't have an answer for her. I did wonder if between us we could come up with some way of driving Sean McGilligan out of the district, to go and sell his honey in the big market in Donegal Town. But let alone I couldn't think of a way of doing this, it didn't seem very fair either. Sean was a man I couldn't help liking, with his jokes and his friendly ways. And sure he'd as much right as Peggy to sell his honey nearer home, without having to go miles away.

I promised Peggy I'd do my best to think of something, and over the next few days I racked my brains, but with no result. Then I happened to meet up with Sean one evening at the *Golden Pheasant*, and as we sat sharing a pint and a bit of a crack, it came to me that Sean wasn't his usual cheerful self. I suggested we move over to a more private corner of the bar, out of hearing of the rest of the customers. Soon we were sitting at a table in a sheltered nook by the fire, where the nearest person was a fair way off. I worked my way round to it and after a while I was able to ask him what was the matter. Then it all came pouring out.

'Seamus, I thought I'd be able to make a good living from the bees and the honey, but every week thon crater Peggy Coyle has her price lower again, so I have to cut mine even further. If this goes on I'll be so broke I'll be not just in pieces but ground to dust! I just don't know what to do.'

I couldn't help laughing. It seemed to me there was an easy way out. It was a mystery why neither Sean nor Peggy had thought of it yet.

'Why don't you go into partnership?' I suggested to him. 'That way you can put the price back up to something reasonable and both of you do well.'

But Sean wouldn't hear of it.

'What, be partners with that Peggy Coyle? Not a chance! If ever I met a proud, stuck up selfish woman it's Peggy Coyle. She thinks she's not just the bees' knees, but the very Queen bee, herself! The things she's said to me, you wouldn't believe, and the names she's called me – I don't know where she's picked them up – not from me, anyway,' Sean finished virtuously.

I couldn't help laughing.

'Sure, I've heard you say some hard things to the lady yourself, Sean,' I reminded him. But I couldn't make him change his mind. And when I came to think of it, it seemed a bit unlikely that Peggy would be any keener on a partnership than Sean was.

All the same I put it to her, but with much the same response. Peggy stuck her nose in the air, and declared that she'd rather be in her grave than in partnership with a big loud-mouthed lout like that Sean McGilligan.

I changed the subject hastily before she started on me as well.

'Talking of graves, Peggy,' I said, 'I suppose you'll be going to put flowers on your parents' grave this week? It's the anniversary of your Da's death, isn't it?'

'It is, Seamus.' A tear stole down Peggy's cheek. 'I still miss them, you know.'

I said no more, but a thought came to me, and that night I called round with Sean and dropped a hint or two.

Next morning, I took a stroll round to the graveyard and kept myself out of sight behind a nearby grave with a huge Angel on it, just hoping.

Sure enough, presently here came Peggy with a bunch of roses in her hand. She put them down by her father's grave. Then she went off to get some fresh water for the jar she kept there.

I heard another set of footsteps coming near and I took a quick look out past the angel. There was Sean McGilligan with another bunch of roses – white by contrast to Peggy's red – and a vase in his other hand. He set the flowers down and made off in turn to the water tap. I stole a bit nearer, to see what would happen.

Peggy had just finished filling her jar when Sean came up with her. She turned her back on him and walked away. But it didn't take Sean long to get his water and by the time she was halfway through arranging her flowers, he was back at the grave beside her. She said nothing until she saw him lift the white roses and stick them haphazard into his vase, then she gave an exclamation.

'Are those from you, Sean?'

'They are,' said Sean. 'Your Da was a good friend to me, Peggy, in many a way. It was him lent me the money for my fare to America, years ago. I paid it back, mind, as soon as I'd earned enough. I didn't come home in time to see him again. But I like to remember him.'

'I've seen the roses here for the past couple of years, Sean,' said Peggy shyly. 'But I didn't know it was you brought them.'

Sean said nothing at first. Then, a bit awkwardly, 'You must miss them both, Peggy.'

'Yes.' Peggy's tears began in good earnest. 'Here, give me those!' she said, trying to recover. She took the roses and the vase from Sean and rearranged the flowers. Then she set them down by her own, and wiped furiously at her tears.

Sean produced a big clean handkerchief from his pocket and leaned over her. Putting one arm round her shoulder, he carefully blotted up her tears.

'You and me should be better friends, Peggy,' he said. 'I don't know why we got off on the wrong foot – I never intended to set up as a rival to you.'

Then he leaned over Peggy a bit further and gave her an anxious sort of a smile.

Well, I wasn't sure what to expect. I'd known Sean had been leaving flowers at Paddy Coyle's grave for the couple of years since he'd been home, for I'd seen him at it. But Peggy might never have seen him in another ten years if they'd been left to themselves, for Sean had a habit of going there brave and early, while she left it till the afternoon as a rule. So when I'd called on Sean the evening before, I'd suggested that he should make his visit to Paddy's grave a bit later than usual.

But as to how Peggy would take it, I didn't know. What I was hoping for was that they might make friends, and decide that they could manage the partnership I'd suggested, after all.

But I got more than I'd bargained for. For when Sean bent over Peggy with his arm round her shoulder to wipe away her tears, didn't she fling her arms round his neck, and lift her face up to his, and a moment later they were kissing as if they'd never stop.

I could see clearly, as I crept quietly away, that it wasn't just going to be a business partnership between them.

And sure enough, they were married only a few weeks later, and before long the price of honey went up again in Millerstown market. But I, for one, was quite happy about that.

4 The Mysterious Gift

As I struggled through the haze of snowflakes, blown directly into my face by the sharp east wind, I wondered if I was mad to come out on such a wild afternoon when I didn't need to. I could have stayed cosily content, stretched out in front of my warm fire, in my little white-washed cottage in the small Donegal village of Ardnakil.

But I had promised myself the pleasure, during this short winter break from my busy city job, of bringing a certain present to my old friend Seamus O'Hare, and I couldn't resist going to see him without further delay.

I'd known Seamus since I used to come to Ardnakil as a child to visit my grandparents. A lovable rogue who lived mainly by poaching, Seamus had taught me everything I knew about the countryside, and had told me countless stories about the people, mostly friends of his – and some enemies! – who lived there. I always enjoyed catching up with him when I came back to Ardnakil to stay in the cottage which had been left to me by my grandparents some years ago.

I almost missed Seamus's tumbledown old cottage when I reached it, blinded as I was by the snow, and it was only when I heard a voice calling my name that I realised I was there. Seamus had come out to his front door to scatter crumbs for the birds and to wipe the snow from his bird table, and he saw me stumbling past his gate.

'Jamie! Come in out of the cold, why don't you?'

'Seamus! Am I glad to see you?' I responded. 'I was coming to call in on you. I nearly missed my way.'

A few moments later I was settled comfortably in one of Seamus's huge dilapidated armchairs in front of his glowing turf fire, a mug of Seamus's home made soup clasped in my rapidly thawing hands and a beam of satisfaction on my face.

'This is great, Seamus,' I sighed in content. 'And as soon as my hands are properly thawed out, I have a surprise present in my pocket to give you.'

'A surprise, Jamie? Well, now, there's nothing I love so much as a surprise present! And I think most people feel like that, too. The surprise is a big part of the pleasure, isn't it?'

I laughed. 'Oh, it's nothing very great. In fact, I hope you won't be disappointed, after this build up.' I set my mug of soup down carefully on the floor beside me, and fished in my pocket. 'Here it is.'

Seamus took the wrapped parcel from my hands and began at once to open it, his face a picture of delight and expectation.

'A book. Why, Jamie! It's a book written by yourself! Man dear, if that's not wonderful! I couldn't be better pleased! And this is a copy for me?'

'Indeed it is, Seamus. You know I've been writing odds and ends of articles for one of the newspapers for the past few years – a bit of a break from business. And now they've been published in book form. I'm pretty pleased about it myself.'

Seamus was turning the pages, exclaiming, reading bits aloud. 'Boy's a dear, you couldn't have given me a present I'd be better pleased with. I'll enjoy reading this, I can tell you. I'll start into it properly at bedtime tonight. I love a good read before I go to sleep. And to think of you keeping it to surprise me with! Sure, some surprises are not too nice, but a surprise present is nearly always a great pleasure.' He put the book down beside him and gave me one of his mischievous grins, his eyes twinkling between the laughter lines on his brown, wrinkled old face. 'Did I ever tell you about the surprise present my friend Agnes Clare was given, a long time ago now?'

'If it's one of your stories, Seamus, go ahead and tell it to me now,' I said sleepily. The warmth of the fire and the soup were having their inevitable effect on me.

'Well, drink up your soup while it's still warm and get some heat into you, boy, and I'll surely tell you,' said Seamus, settling back comfortably into the other big armchair.

Aggie Clare lived by herself, at the time I'm speaking of. Her parents were dead and her sister had married young and moved to Dublin. Aggie was still quite young herself. She had a nice wee job working behind the bar in the *Golden Pheasant*, and many's the good chat I used to have with her when I called in there.

Mind you, it was hard enough to get near her sometimes, for Aggie was a good looking youngster and the young fellows were round her like bees round the flowers looking for honey.

There was one young fellow in particular that she seemed to like better than the rest, by name Rory Duggan. Rory was a wild, reckless youngster from up the country. His father had been a feckless sort of a critter and had let the farm he'd inherited from Rory's granda go to wrack and ruin, so that there wasn't much left of it by the time it came to Rory. Many's a time I heard Rory say he'd be off to Dublin to make some money in a decent job before long. But it was plain enough what was keeping him back, and that was Aggie Clare.

So it was no great surprise to anyone when Rory and Aggie began smiling and whispering, and at last letting out the secret that they were all fixed to get married as soon as Father Donegan could do the job for them.

Well so, engaged to be married they were, and to all appearances very happy. But under the surface there was trouble brewing. Aggie told me all about it later, but at the time I was as flummoxed as anyone when the next we heard was that Rory had taken himself off to Dublin after all, and that everything was over between him and Aggie.

Aggie told me what the trouble was one evening, when we were alone in the bar, for I'd come in and found her bawling her eyes out. It seemed that Rory had a wide streak of jealousy in him.

'You know what it's like for me working here behind the bar, Seamus,' Aggie wept. 'There's a many young fellows in and out and most of them want to flirt with me and get a kind word or a smile, but every time I talked to one of them Rory lost the rag. He'd maybe say little right then, but later on when he was walking me home he'd start in on me, giving off a bucketful.

I tried to be reasonable at first. I can see his point, sure. But it was getting so I could hardly open my mouth without him shouting at me afterwards, so then I started shouting back, until one time I told him if he didn't like me the way I am, he could just take himself off, for I wasn't going to marry him after all!'

Aggie gave an enormous sob, and I patted her hand – looking round to make sure Rory wasn't there watching me.

'Sure, it sounds to me like the sort of row most young couples have, Aggie. He should know you didn't mean it.'

'Well, indeed I didn't, Seamus. But now he's gone off to Dublin, and I'll never see him again!'

It was a problem, all right.

'How do you know he's in Dublin, Aggie?' I asked her.

'He sent me a postcard with his address on it. Maybe he thinks I'll write and ask him to come back – but there's no way I'm doing that! He needs to say he's sorry and change his ways first, Seamus.'

So I could see it was stalemate.

Just then young Tommy McMordie came into the *Golden Pheasant*, and Aggie hastily dried her eyes and put on her professional face. Tommy, a nice young lad, was one of the fellows really keen on Aggie, and seeing him talking to her gave me an idea. Rory was gone. Maybe Tommy could make up to Aggie for losing him? But I wasn't sure if there was anything I could do about it.

Tommy and I walked home after closing time that evening, and I could see he'd something on his mind. Sure enough, after hm'ming and ha'hing for a bit, he finally spoke up.

'Seamus, could you put in a word for me with Aggie Clare? You and Aggie are good friends, aren't you? Maybe she'd listen to you.'

'Sure, why should you need me to speak for you, Tommy, boy? Tell her yourself how you feel about her. That's always the best way,' I said.

'Aw, many's the time I've tried, Seamus,' Tommy confessed, looking right and miserable. 'But I'm so used to bantering and joking with her, I can't seem to be serious. I can't find the right words.'

'Well, I'll put in a word for you, Tommy, if you really want me to. But a girl always thinks better of a man if he speaks up for himself.'

'Do you think so, Seamus? Well, maybe you'd better say nothing just yet, and I'll see if I can speak for myself, as you say.'

But as the days passed, Tommy seemed more and more unable to come to the point with Aggie.

Then one day Tommy's chances were blown away, because when I ran into Aggie coming out of her cottage I saw at once that something had happened. She was beaming all over her face, and she had a half unwrapped parcel in her hand.

'Seamus, Seamus, look what Rory's sent me!' she burst out, thrusting the parcel at me.

It was a book of poetry, and inside the cover there was a card which said, 'This will tell you what I want to say to you.'

There was no name signed.

'And what makes you think it was Rory sent it?' I asked cautiously.

'Well, sure, you can see from the postmark it came from Dublin!' Aggie looked at me as if I was stupid. 'I'm going to the village to get some writing paper and envelopes and stamps, and I'm going to write to him straight-away,' she went on. 'Though, mind you, Seamus, I'm for telling him he needs to stop all this jealous nonsense, if he wants to come back. But fancy Rory being so romantic!'

'The whole thing's a bit of a mystery, Aggie. And if you'll take some advice from an old friend, I think you shouldn't mention the book when you write to Rory.'

'Why on earth not?' Aggie asked me.

'Well, you never know. If it wasn't him, you might just start him off being jealous again.'

It took a lot of persuading, but in the end I got her to agree not to mention it.

'But if it wasn't Rory, sure I wouldn't write to him at all, Seamus!'

'Oh, you go ahead and write, Aggie,' I said quickly. 'The last thing I want is to stop you doing that! And maybe you shouldn't tell anyone else about it – Rory might be embarrassed, supposing it was Rory who sent it.'

So write she did, and shortly afterwards there was Rory back home again, and the pair of them all smiles. The wedding was on again, and very soon they were settled down together. Aggie stopped smiling so much at the other fellows, and Rory managed to control his temper a lot better, so I daresay they were as happy as any other young married couple.

The one who wasn't so happy was Tommy McMordie.

He came grumbling to me one evening.

'To think of the money I wasted ordering that book for Aggie all the way from the Dublin bookseller, Seamus!' was the main subject of his complaint. 'I thought for sure it would do the job. And I even took the trouble to get them to include a message in it!'

'Ah, but you didn't sign it, Tommy,' I pointed out to him gently.

'I thought a surprise would be more romantic, Seamus. I was going to tell her it was from me as soon as she mentioned it. But there was never a word out of her about it. And then there was that Rory Duggan back again and my hopes down the drain.'

I was sorry for the boy, but I couldn't help saying, 'Well, Tommy – books of poetry are nice, but if you don't dare tell a girl to her face that you love her, you can't expect to get very far. Talking about poetry, I remember a few lines I learnt at school.

'He either fears his fate too much, or his deserts are small,
Who dare not put it to the touch, to win or lose it all!'

And there's an old proverb, too. '*Faint heart never won fair lady!*'

What did I tell you when you asked my advice, not long ago? I didn't tell you to send Aggie a mystery gift that could have been from anybody. I told you, Tommy lad, that you needed to learn how to speak up for yourself!'

5 Liam's Birthday Balloons

The sun was smiling happily down on the green grass of Ardnakil as I strolled, hands in my trouser pockets, past the open front garden of a pleasant house on the edge of the little Donegal village. I was on holiday, without a care in the world, relaxing in the small, whitewashed cottage my grand-parents had left me some years ago, and I was just out for a dander in the warm summer air. It was good to get away from the city, and from city life, for a short break.

There were shrieks of merriment coming from the garden as I passed it, and I couldn't help taking a glance over the low hedge to see what was going on. The grass was covered in bright, coloured shapes which gave the eye a fleeting impression of dozens of scattered flowers, but which on a second glance turned out to be a crowd of very young children, mostly around five or six. They were running in all directions chasing the multi-coloured balloons which were being batted through the air for them to catch by – yes, I looked again, it was definitely him – my old friend, Seamus O'Hare.

I stood watching for a minute and presently a birthday cake appeared from the house, carried on a silver stand by an excited lady, obviously the mother of at least one of the children. A moment later Seamus, mopping his forehead with a red silk handkerchief, slipped unobtrusively out through the open gate, and leaned against the hedge, breathing a sigh of relief. It took him a few seconds to recover his breath enough to notice me.

'Jamie, my boy! Great to see you!'

'What on earth are you up to, Seamus?'

The bright eyes twinkled in Seamus's wrinkled, brown old face and he ran one hand through his curly white hair as he gave me one of his mischievous grins.

'Just adding my mite to the birthday celebrations, Jamie my boy. Wee Terry is a mate of mine and I've known his mother Agnes since she was Terry's age – which is exactly six today. And sure, what's a birthday party without balloons? So I just thought I'd bring some along.'

'That was a nice idea, Seamus. But you shouldn't be dashing about like that at your age!'

'Less of the 'your age,' boy,' Seamus retorted. 'There's life in the old dog yet! Mind you, I think I'll bow out now. How about you and me popping along to the *Golden Pheasant* for a jar?'

As he spoke a bright red balloon came floating over the hedge between us, and I reached up and caught it.

'I used to love these things when I was a kid,' I said reflectively. 'You're right, Seamus, a birthday party wouldn't be the same without them.'

'I have an old friend who'd fully agree with you on that, Jamie,' Seamus said. He said no more for a moment, but when we reached the local pub, the *Golden Pheasant*, and settled ourselves at a table with a cool pint each, he went on, 'I'll tell you about her if you like.'

I enjoy Seamus's stories. And it seems that whenever we meet he has another one ready for me.

'Go ahead, Seamus,' I said, laughing. 'I'm listening.'

Seamus grinned at me, took out his disreputable old pipe, and lit up. Then he began.

It was a few years ago, Seamus said, that I ran into Bella Maloney in the village, and she told me that she and her husband Willy had come back here to live, now Willy was retired. I'd known her when we were children together at the same village school, but she'd married and moved away long since.

'My daughter Sarah and her husband Mike have just bought a cottage nearby, Seamus. Well, when I say nearby, it's out past the Errigal mountain,' Bella told me. 'She said she's heard me rabbiting on for most of her life about what a great place Donegal was for kids to grow up in, so she and Mike had to come and see for themselves!'

I looked around me at the nearby hills, dressed in green, at the cow parsley lining the lanes like bridal veils, at the honeysuckle sweetly scenting the air, at the river chuckling its way down past the millpond and under the bridge in the middle of the village, and above all at the wide open green spaces where children could run freely. I watched a blackbird with its bright orange beak settle itself in the apple tree in my friend Annie's cottage garden, which was just in sight, and I listened as it began its melodious song. And I couldn't help agreeing. There couldn't be anywhere better for a child to grow up in the whole of God's green earth.

'And does she have kiddies, then, Bella?' I asked.

'Just the one, so far, Seamus. A real wee dote. He's called Liam after Willy – wasn't that nice of them?'

'Well, that's great, Bella. Now you be sure and spoil him rotten, won't you – after all, that's what grannies are for!'

And from all accounts, that was exactly what Bella and Willy did. It seemed there was nothing they wouldn't do for Liam. In fact, I felt I should give Bella a word of warning not to take my joke too seriously about spoiling the boy. Only grandson or not, there had to be limits to what she was prepared to do.

I told her so, but she only laughed at me.

'Sure, wee Liam deserves the very best, Seamus,' she said. 'And I mean to see that he gets it!'

It came round after a while to young Liam's sixth birthday, and Bella was all out to make it the most special birthday ever. Sarah was having a party for the child, naturally, and as well as buying him most of the contents of the local toyshops, Bella promised she and Willy would go along on the day and help as much as they could.

On the birthday afternoon, Sarah phoned her mammy in a bit of a state. It seemed that young Liam had suddenly come out with a request for balloons at his party – the one thing Sarah hadn't thought of.

'Balloons, Sarah?' Bella said. 'Right, pet. Our grandson can't be without balloons on his sixth birthday. Daddy and me'll bring some, okay?'

'Mammy, you're an angel!' said Sarah's fervent voice from the other end of the phone. 'See you three-ish, then. Or even earlier!'

Bella turned round to Willy.

'Sarah forgot to buy balloons! We'll have to get some.'

'Okay,' said Willy placidly. He was never the man to get into a flap. 'Have you got the camera, Bella love?'

'Och, Willy, thank goodness you remembered!'

They were heading out of the house and getting into Willy's ramshackle old Austin car by then, so Bella jumped out of the car, ran into the house, and rushed back with the camera dangling from her arm by its strap.

'There must be at least three shops selling balloons, on the way to Sarah's cottage, Willy. We should be able to get what we want easy enough.'

'Like, balloons.'

'Oh, but we want ones with 'Happy Birthday!' on them!' Bella insisted. 'And his age, if possible. And maybe even his name.'

The first shop had balloons with 'Happy Birthday,' but no names or ages.

'Sure, just get a packet of those'uns, Bella love,' Willy encouraged her. 'He'll like all the different colours.'

But, no, Bella was determined only to get balloons which were really special. They hurried out of the shop. Time was going on.

The second shop, miles further on, had no 'Happy Birthday' balloons. Finally Bella found some with '6 years old today!'

But they were pink.

'Wee Liam won't know any better,' Willy said reasonably.

'No, but sure you know Mike would never stand for it,' Bella protested.

They both thought about their very macho son-in-law. Pink balloons for his six year old son. No way.

'Well, there's still one more shop before we get there,' Willy said resignedly.

'One more yet,' Bella agreed optimistically. 'We'll surely get the right sort there.'

They reached the last possible shop, on the outskirts of the nearest village to where Sarah and Mike lived. A sign said, 'Moved to New Premises.'

It was almost three o'clock.

'We can't go back,' said Willy decidedly. 'You know we promised Sarah we'd be there on time. She needs us to help cope with all these kids she's invited, with or without balloons.'

Bella had to acknowledge that Willy, as usual, was right.

'If only we hadn't been so fussy!' she moaned. ' Sure, any balloons would do now. We should have taken those ones in the first shop, even though they didn't have his age on. After all, they were specially for birthdays.'

Willy, a man happily married for many years, and one who had learnt a lot during that time, carefully said nothing, and they drove on.

They had spent so much time already that Bella's watch showed two minutes to three, with several miles still to go. They turned off the main road onto a narrow lane running round the foot of the mountain between wild hedges of fuchsia and some fragile wild roses, which would eventually take them to Sarah's cottage. They were halfway round Mount Errigal when suddenly Bella noticed something.

'Sweetheart! Pull over!'

There at the side of the lane, tied to the gateposts of a long winding drive, the house hidden by bushes along its length, were balloons.

Heaps of balloons. Red balloons, yellow balloons, white balloons, green balloons, blue balloons. It seemed that someone else was having a birthday.

Bella made up her mind quickly. There were so many balloons here! They could spare some!

'Wait, Willy! Stop the car!' she ordered. 'I'm going to get some of those balloons!'

Willy obeyed automatically, but couldn't help protesting. 'But, pet –' he began. But he was speaking to thin air.

Bella had already leapt out of the car, sprinting back along the grassy verge, to where the many coloured balloons bobbed and beckoned invitingly in the warm little breeze. She looked round furtively. Yes, the gateposts were well out of sight of the house.

Feverishly she wrestled with the strings attaching the balloons to the nearest gatepost. If only she had scissors, she thought. Better still, wire-cutters. She felt like an escapee breaking out from a prisoner-of-war camp.

Success! Some of the strings had come undone.

Seizing as many balloons as possible, Bella headed back to the car at double-quick speed.

A shout echoed behind her.

An enormous man with a face like a gorilla was emerging from the driveway.

'Quick!' Bella yelled, diving headlong into the car. 'Go, go, go!'

They went.

Willy was a careful driver, as a rule, but this time he broke the speed limit and then some.

Bella looked round. Surely they were leaving pursuit far behind?

No!

A heavy four-wheel-drive thundered after the little Austin. Behind the wheel, Bella could see that gorilla-like face.

Round bend after bend they roared franticly, scattering the petals from the late wild roses in the hedges, swerving to avoid the banks of buttercups along the lane's edges.

'It's no use, love,' panted Willy. 'The poor old car's giving up. We can't outdrive him in that monster.'

Bella looked down sadly at her gaily-coloured booty. What a fuss about a few balloons!

Willy pulled in, to the side to the lane, and stopped the car.

The four-wheel-drive stopped behind them and the gorilla man climbed out.

Willy bravely opened the window, while Bella shrank back in her seat.

'I think you dropped something back there,' the man said. He held out something to Bella, something dangling on the end of a strap. 'Is this your camera?'

Well, all was well that ended well. To Bella's surprised delight, the man wasn't interested in the balloons at all. So Bella got her camera back, and wee Liam got his birthday balloons.

But Bella told me afterwards that she'd learnt a lesson that day which she'd never forget – that there's no use trying to be kind to someone by stealing from someone else. Even if you don't get found out, the guilt alone makes the whole thing such a nightmare that there's no way it's worth risking!

6 Seamus Takes A Ride

'When I was a youngster,' my old friend Seamus O'Hare told me thought-fully, sucking at his disreputable old pipe, 'there weren't so many of these cars flying about the roads.'

We had just crossed the main street, such as it was, of the little Donegal village of Ardnakil, where Seamus lived and where I came, as a visitor, as often as I could, to stay in the small, whitewashed cottage my grandparents left me. It was when we were halfway across that a huge monster of a car, horn blaring furiously, swept past us in a cloud of dust, narrowly missing us both and forcing us to jump for our lives.

We stood, dusting ourselves off and recovering, on the other side of the road.

'I remember the first motor car I ever saw,' said Seamus, his brown wrinkled face creasing in smiles and his bright eyes twinkling. He brushed the curly white hair back from his forehead. 'If you'd like to walk along the river bank and find somewhere peaceful to sit, Jamie lad, I'll tell you about it.'

'I well remember the times when cars were more unusual, even in the city, Seamus,' I replied. 'When I was a youngster, we could play foot-ball in the street. Nowadays, you'd be mowed down in seconds if you tried it.'

We crossed the bridge over the river which ran along beside the village street of Ardnakil, and walked along the river bank until we left the last cottage behind us, and came into a lush green area of fields and trees. There we found a quiet place and sat down under a green-leaved chestnut tree, with its creamy, shining candles upright on every branch.

We lay back against the grassy riverbank. I clasped my hands behind my head and breathed in the country smell of honeysuckle and clover. The river chuckled joyously as it bounded over rocks and stones, with a swish of white frills to decorate the clear green silken water. I smiled in deep content, and prepared to listen to another of Seamus's stories.

And Seamus, chewing a piece of grass as he spoke, told me about the first time he ever saw a motorcar.

Well, Jamie, he began, you won't be surprised to hear that the first car I ever saw, a long open topped Bentley, very red and shiny and to my infant eyes enormous, came to Ardnakil to the big house. Now, it didn't belong to the Hon. Marjorie Fitzpatrick herself, nor yet to her father, Gerald Fitzpatrick, who was still alive at the time. It belonged to a visitor, and, as I had already learnt, a visitor who wasn't exactly a friend. He was a business acquaintance, a hard man called Terence O'Hagan who had had serious business dealings with the Hon. Marjorie's father.

I happened to hear the Hon Marjorie and her father talking about him one day, when I'd been tickling a fish or two in their river, as they came towards me, walking along the bank.

'You know, Marjorie, the same man lent me a heap of money, with Carmarnoc House as surety,' said Lord Fitzpatrick, 'and now he's talking of calling the loan in.'

'But sure, how can he do that, Father? Isn't there an agreement that you have so many years to pay it back?'

'Well, no, Marjorie, there isn't. But you know there would be no problem paying the loan back if only Terence O'Hagan would stick to the original gentleman's agreement, and give me a bit of grace.'

'Yes,' said the Hon Marjorie, 'I know you're expecting a right big sum as an inheritance from your great aunt Eileen, who can't last many more years, being ninety-eight next birthday.'

'Och, it would be much more than enough to cover the loan and put us back on our feet,' Lord Fitzpatrick said. 'But Terence O'Hagan wants Carmarnoc House. He'd rather have that than the money. He knows there's no way I'd sell him the property – it's been in our family for hundreds of years. Since there was no date in the I.O.U. he can call it in whenever he wants. And he's given me notice that that's what he plans to do.'

I had heard enough, and as they moved away past me I slid carefully out of the bushes and made my way home. But although I usually had little sympathy for the well off landed gentry in this country, I couldn't help feeling a bit sorry for the Fitzpatricks. This man Terence O'Hagan would be a much worse person to have living at the big house, from the sound of him.

It was a few weeks later, and I'd almost forgotten the matter, when the shiny red Bentley made its way through the village and headed up towards Carmarnoc House.

Everyone was talking about it, and I soon heard from Maggie O'Hara who worked up there that it belonged to a visitor called O'Hagan.

Well, that might have been the end of it.

But the Bentley was the first car I'd ever seen, so when next day I saw it parked not far from the *Golden Pheasant* in the village street, I could no more have resisted going over for a closer look than I could have flown.

I don't know what spark of mischief put it into my head, but I felt a great urge to climb in and see how it felt to sit in one of these new contraptions. I'd have dearly loved a ride in it, but that didn't seem at all likely. Until it happened.

Two men came out of the *Golden Pheasant* and walked towards the car.

It was too late for me to scramble out of the car and get away without being caught. The best I could do was to clamber into the back and crouch down with the car rug hiding me, as they both got in.

And a moment later I was getting my wish for a ride in the Bentley, for one of the men started up the car and suddenly we were off down the village street.

'Terence,' said the one who wasn't driving, 'this is a great wee car you have here.'

'Not so bad,' said the other man – who must be the Terence O'Hagan I'd heard mentioned. 'But, getting down to business, Michael, have you done anything about that matter we talked about?'

Michael, who from what I'd seen of him was a thin, elderly man with a prim air about him, said, 'Yes, I've looked into it, Terence. I think I can make it work.'

'Good.' O'Hagan, I'd noticed, was a stout, red-faced man with thinning dark hair and an unpleasant expression. 'So, you've arranged to leak the story that there's no oil in the Peruvian Oilfields, and the shares are worthless?'

'I have that, Terence,' said Michael. 'But, as your lawyer, I have to warn you that what you're up to is dangerous. If anyone heard that you'd leaked a made up report to bring the share prices down, so you could buy them up yourself, you could be arrested. You'd certainly be ruined in the city.'

'Now, how would anyone find that out, Michael?' purred O'Hagan. 'Not by you telling them, sure! For you're just as much involved as me, and you'll be buying up the shares too, to sell them again and make a fortune, when people realise there was no truth in the rumour and the prices go back up!'

I wasn't very old at the time, you realise, Jamie, but I knew enough to understand that the two men were plotting to make money on the Stock Exchange by underhand, dishonest methods. I was disgusted with them, and I was wondering what I should do, when the car turned out onto a main road and put on a bit of speed.

We'd already been travelling at a rate which seemed to me amazingly fast, since the quickest thing I'd ever been in up until then was a donkey and cart, but now it seemed as if the wind was whistling past me and the Bentley might take off and fly at any minute.

'Do you think you'll get me to the station in time to catch this train, Terence?' the lawyer asked, and I realised that they were headed to the railway station in Millerstown.

'Certainly, me boyo!' O'Hagan said boastfully. 'This car can't be beaten! I'll get you to your train in plenty of time, and be back at Carmarnoc House in ample time to change for dinner!'

So I sat back and enjoyed my first car ride, with the green hedges zooming past me at a terrific speed, and I felt thankful that soon one of the men would be getting out, and I'd only have O'Hagan to deal with. Two of them might have been too much to handle, but I could surely cope with one.

For I'd made up my mind that I wasn't just going to hide until O'Hagan got back to Ardnakil, and then try to escape without being seen. It seemed to me that this unpleasant man deserved a shock, and if I could manage it I was going to give him one.

The Bentley drove rather more slowly through the streets of Millerstown and pulled up in front of the huge, impressive looking structure which was Millerstown Railway Station. The lawyer got out. He had a small overnight case which he must have left in the front of the car when he and O'Hagan stopped at the *Golden Pheasant.* He had been carrying it on his knee since they got back in. I could only be thankful he hadn't left it in the back of the car, for he'd have been sure to see me when he collected it.

'Well, bye-bye, Terence,' he said. 'I'll see about that business tomorrow, if I don't hear from you.' With a wave of his hand he disappeared into the station. O'Hagan turned the car round, and in no time at all we were flying back along the road.

It was just before we reached Ardnakil that I decided the time had come for action.

Standing up in the back of the car, I said in a loud voice, 'Mr O'Hagan!'

The car jerked, swerved, and came to a sudden halt with its nose almost in the nearest hedge.

'What? What?' quavered O'Hagan, in a very different voice from the one I'd heard him use when he was speaking to his lawyer.

'I need to speak to you, Mr O'Hagan,' I said firmly. 'Turn round and look at me!'

O'Hagan swivelled round in his seat, his eyes starting out of his head and his red cheeks white with terror. But when he saw that the voice which had scared him belonged to a boy, his face quickly grew red again with anger.

'What do you mean by getting into my car, you wee hallion?' he roared. 'I'll hand you over to the police when I get you back to Ardnakil!'

'Well, I think you might be sorry if you did that, Mr. O'Hagan,' I said. 'Because I heard everything you and your friend Michael were saying about Peruvian Oil. If the police come into this, you're the one who'll be in the worst trouble.'

O'Hagan's face began to pale again rapidly. 'What do you mean?' he asked in a trembling whisper.

'I mean you could go to prison, as you well know!'

'You mustn't tell!' O'Hagan cried. 'Look – I'll give you anything you want! Here – ' he began to pull banknotes out of his wallet – 'how much will it take to keep you quiet?'

'I don't want money,' I told him. 'But there are two things I want you to do.'

'Just tell me! I'll do them!'

'Firstly,' I said, 'tell your lawyer to cancel the plans to leak that rumour. I don't see why you should get away with cheating a whole lot of people just to make money yourself.'

O'Hagan looked stricken, but he nodded. 'All right. And what's the second thing?'

'You've been threatening to call in the loan you made to Lord Fitz-patrick and take his house. I don't think much of Lord Fitzpatrick, but I think even less of you, Mr O'Hagan. Draw up a document giving Lord Fitzpatrick another ten years before the loan becomes due.' (I reckoned his Great Aunt Eileen could hardly stick it out for more than another ten years, her being ninety-eight!) 'And don't think you can agree and then break your word. Because I can still report what I heard, remember!'

Well, the long and the short of it was that O'Hagan agreed, and the Fitz-patricks got to keep Carmarnoc House. They never knew what I'd done for them. To tell you the truth, many a time, when they gave me grief about taking the odd fish from their waters, I wondered why I'd bothered! But years afterwards when I got to be friends with the Hon Marjorie over that business of Annie's apple tree, I was glad I'd done it. She's not a bad old girl, really, the Hon Marjorie!

7 The Christmas Present

Christmas was almost upon us when I took the opportunity of a few days break, before plunging into the usual family visits, and escaped up to my small country cottage in the little Donegal village of Ardnakil. The weather was mild for the season. This wasn't going to be a white Christmas, whatever might happen later in the year.

As soon as I had settled in and unpacked my few belongings, I headed out for a stroll, in the pleasant sunny air of late afternoon, towards the tumbledown old cottage where my friend Seamus O'Hare lives.

Seamus is someone I've known since my childhood, when I came up to visit my grandparents in that same cottage which I've now inherited. Seamus, a disreputable old poacher, made a living selling fish he'd acquired from the Lisnakil river to the local pubs and restaurants, as well as pheasants from the woods belonging to the big house. At this time of year, his poaching activities were cut down, and I found him, as I'd expected, sitting comfortably in one of his shabby, but cosy, armchairs in front of a glowing turf fire.

'Ah, come away in, Jamie!' he greeted me, 'and sit yourself down by the fire, boy!'

'I brought you a wee Christmas present, Seamus,' I said. 'Nothing much – just a few Guinness to repay you for all the pints you've bought for me at the *Golden Pheasant.*'

'Och, you're a marvel, boyo!' Seamus said, standing up to take the box of 24 Guinness I'd manhandled along his cottage lane. 'We'll broach this now, and not keep it for Christmas.' And he opened the box and handed me a can, taking one himself.

'Christmas presents – they're a great idea,' he said presently, when we were both comfortably settled by the glowing turf fire, with its beguiling smell which always evoked for me the memory of Ireland past. 'But they can be a real problem sometimes. I remember the trouble my young friend Patsy Adair had with one special present, a good few years ago.'

'So, tell me the story, Seamus.'

'If you like, Jamie.' Seamus settled himself more comfortably, stretched out his feet to the warmth of the fire, and began.

‘Patsy was a good wee girl, kindness itself to the wild creatures she came across in the woods and fields. She couldn’t resist taking an injured bird or rabbit home with her to nurse, and her wee cottage was full of stray dogs and cats. She spent most of the money she earned, working as a waitress at the *Golden Pheasant*, in buying food for her invalids or paying the vet’s bills. The result was that Patsy was usually a bit hard up, but I never heard her complaining.

I was delighted, and so were all Patsy’s many friends, when young Peter Hennessy began to pay her a bit of attention, dropping in to the *Golden Pheasant* a lot, and inviting her to come for walks or to the pictures in Millerstown.

Peter was a nice young lad, with a good job at Millerstown Library. There was only one thing less than perfect about him as a suitor for Patsy – his mother. Peter’s father, like Patsy’s own parents, had died when Peter was in his late teens, and he still lived with his mother, mainly, I thought, because he believed she’d be miserable and lonely if he moved out. Maire Hennessy was a very bossy, possessive sort of a woman, and it was my own idea that she made Peter’s life a bit of a misery to him, keeping a strict eye on his friends and the places he went to. Not that I ever heard Peter say so, mind you. He and Patsy were a matching pair – neither of them was the type to grumble. They just got on with their lives.

Well, the two of them had been going out a few months, and it was getting near to Christmas, when Peter decided it was time to take the plunge and bring Patsy home to meet his mother. And when he mentioned this to Maire Hennessy, she put on a big smile and said she would invite Patsy to the Christmas party she always held for family and friends, the day before Christmas Eve.

Peter was a bit dismayed.

‘Patsy might be a bit shy about that, Mammy,’ he protested. ‘I wanted to bring her round some time when it was just you on your own, so you could get to know each other. Not a whole big family social gathering!’

‘Och, nonsense, Peter,’ said Maire briskly. ‘The wee girl would be bored stiff if it was just you and me. This way, she can have a good time and enjoy herself. Meet some other young men, even – there’s Annie’s Steven and Peggy’s Michael, for a start.’

And Peter didn’t like to say that Patsy wasn’t looking for any other young man, for Maire was obviously closing her eyes to the fact that Patsy was more than a friend, and that her son had serious intentions towards this particular girl.

So the invitation was given, and as Peter had expected, Patsy was a bit shy about the whole business. She was cleaning out the rabbit hutch where a baby bird with a broken leg was recovering from an attack by either a cat or a fox when the thought suddenly hit her. She would need to bring Peter's mother a present!

Patsy had already bought Peter a book of poetry she knew he'd been longing for, and she was pleased that she'd had enough money to get it. She'd been saving up for a while, cutting down on food for herself, to make sure she had enough for it. Of course, there was no question of cutting down on food for the animals. They always came first, in Patsy's mind.

She finished her task and then scurried into the cottage to check on her savings book. Yes, she might just have enough to buy Maire something. Bath things, or perfume, or an expensive scarf.

She would have to go into Millerstown the next day and pick something really nice.

After tea that night Patsy, as she often did, went for a walk in the woods. It was a beautiful moonlit night. The light shone through the few remaining leaves on the trees, casting exciting shadows across the path where she strolled.

Patsy's thoughts turned, as they usually did these days, to Peter, and how kind and sweet he was. Not many young men these days would stay at home with their widowed mother to keep her company. For to Patsy, this trait in Peter, which I thought of as a bit of a drawback, was a real plus point, highlighting his kind nature. And maybe she was right, at that.

I was out in the woods myself that night – don't ask why – and I ran into Patsy along the path.

'Why, you're out late, girl!' I exclaimed when I saw her. 'Aren't you afraid to be here on your own?'

'No, why should I be, Seamus?' she laughed. 'The animals are all my friends.'

We chatted for a few moments, and it was then that she told me about being invited to Maire's Christmas party. We'd got to the fact that she had just enough money left for Maire's Christmas present when we heard a dreadful shriek.

'A rabbit! In a snare!' Patsy was quick to recognise the sound, as indeed I was myself. I was angry. Although I do a bit of poaching, as you know, I would never dream of setting such cruel traps.

'Let's find it, Seamus!' Patsy cried, and was off like a rocket in the direction of the snare. I followed her just as quickly.

The rabbit was caught by one leg, and unable to get free. It was difficult to calm it down enough to be able to loosen the wire of the snare, but with Patsy's help I managed it. Patsy has a wonderful way with all animals, and her touch seemed to sooth the poor helpless creature. When we had released it, she took it and cradled it in her arms.

'I'll take it home with me, Seamus,' she said in a definite voice. 'Tomorrow when I go into Millerstown I'll call with the vet and see what's needed.'

I didn't attempt to argue with her. I knew what she was like about animals. It was only afterwards I wondered, remembering what she'd been telling me about having just enough money left to buy Maire Hennessy a Christmas present, how she would manage at the vet's.

And sure enough, although the vet held out every hope that the rabbit would recover completely, his charges for treatment left Patsy completely cleaned out. At first she didn't worry. She was too glad that the rabbit would recover to have room in her mind for anything else. But as she rattled home on the old bus, and later as she sat by the fire after making sure all her animals were clean and fed, the thought came creeping over her, filling her with dismay. What was she going to do about a present for Peter's mother?

The party was only two days away. She had no more money coming in – there was no way she could buy anything now. What a dreadful impression she would make, arriving empty handed at Christmas.

Just then a knock came on the door. Going to open it, she was surprised to see an elderly woman whom she knew slightly, Agnes Burke.

'Come away in, Mrs Burke,' Patsy began awkwardly, ushering Agnes into her kitchen. 'Sit down here and I'll pour you a cup of tea – it's just made.'

'Patsy, I just wanted to give you this as a wee thank you for all you did for my kitten that time when she was knocked down on the road. If it hadn't been for you, my wee Frisky wouldn't have survived, the vet said,' Agnes began. She settled herself in the chair by the fire and sipped gratefully at the cup of tea Patsy had thrust at her. 'I couldn't thank you enough. This is just a wee nothing, really. But it comes with my gratitude and my best wishes for a happy and blessed Christmas.' She handed over a beautifully wrapped parcel to Patsy, who took it with exclamations of gratitude.

'Sure, I did nothing, Mrs Burke!' she said. 'All I did was pick up Frisky and get the wound cleaned and bandaged, and ring you and the vet.'

'You may make little of it, but Frisky would have died if you hadn't stopped the bleeding, girl. So I'll always be grateful.'

She stayed for a few more minutes, drinking her tea and looking at all Patsy's rescued animals.

When she eventually went, Patsy breathed a sigh of thankfulness. People being so grateful to her always embarrassed her.

Then she opened her present, and gave a cry of joy. Was this the answer to her prayers? It was a beautiful cashmere scarf, in a distinctive shade of green. Just the thing to give to Maire.

Patsy didn't really like the idea of giving away a present someone had meant for her. But in her difficult position, it seemed the only thing to do.

Until two days later, arriving at Peter's cottage with her scarf freshly wrapped, she went in. And the first person she saw was Agnes Burke. Patsy hadn't known until Peter introduced her that Agnes was Maire Hennessy's aunt.

'Peter – I have to get out!' she whispered to him frantically. How could she give her present to Maire now? Agnes would recognise it at once and be both hurt and angry. She would probably say something!

Patsy ran out of the back door of the cottage, and it was there I found her, weeping her eyes out, with Peter's arm round her shoulder. I'd been worrying about her, and it wasn't just an accident that I happened to pass that way.

Peter and I listened as Patsy wept out her story, then I patted her comfortingly on the arm.

'Don't you be worrying, Patsy,' I said. 'Just give her this instead.'

And I produced from behind my back a pot with three hyacinth bulbs just beginning to show above the soil.

'If she isn't pleased with this, which I grew with my own green fingers, then there's no pleasing her. And as for you spending your money to give a living creature life and freedom again, you should be praised for that, not blamed. Isn't that the true Christmas spirit?'

'Indeed it is, Patsy darlin',' said Peter warmly. 'And it just makes me love you more! Patsy – you're the only girl for me! Will you marry me, sweetheart?'

'Oh, yes, Peter, I will!' breathed Patsy. And they flung their arms round each other and kissed as if the world was coming to an end.

It was the first marriage proposal I'd ever heard in person, and it made me very happy. Even though they went into the house arm in arm to face up to Maire, carrying the pot of hyacinths, without even remembering that I was there!

8 Romance And Father Gillespie

Spring was just round the corner and already the wild crocuses were sprinkling the fields with flashes of bright colour against the new green. I had come up to the little whitewashed cottage I'd inherited from my grandparents, in the small Donegal village of Ardnakil, for a weekend break from my busy city job. On this, my first morning here, the gleams of sunshine beckoned me out, to stroll happily through the fields and woods, enjoying the fresh spring air and the beauty of the countryside.

I half expected, as I walked about at random, to bump into my old friend Seamus O'Hare, and sure enough as I climbed a stile into the next field there he was, strolling along smoking his disreputable old pipe, his blue eyes twinkling in his brown wrinkled old face, his hands in his trouser pockets, and not a care to worry him.

'Jamie, my boy!' he greeted me with a smile. 'Isn't this a morning straight from the youth of the world?'

I've known Seamus since I visited my grandparents as a child, and it was he who showed me how to tickle a trout, and he who identified the flowers, trees and birds for me in response to my eager questions. Now that I'm an adult, I still value Seamus as a good friend and am always delighted to meet up with him again.

'Yes, it's a beautiful day, Seamus,' I answered him. And I must have sighed a little, for Seamus looked at me quizzically.

'A day for thoughts of romance, maybe, boy?'

'Maybe, Seamus.' And before I knew it, I began to tell him about the girl I'd met, and how she seemed to have no interest in me so far.

'Ah, it'll come, boy, it'll come. Sure, in the springtime doesn't everybody think of romance?'

'Not everybody, surely, Seamus?'

'Oh, you'd be surprised!'

I was anxious to turn the conversation away from me, by now. 'Well, not priests, for instance, Seamus?'

‘Maybe not, in the way you mean, Jamie. But there was Father Gillespie, now. His head was full of romantic thoughts, and not just in the springtime, as I found out. But I was the only one who ever knew that.’

‘So, are you going to tell me his story, Seamus?’

‘I might, at that, Jamie. Let’s stroll along as I talk, because, beautiful day or not, the air’s a bit chilly to be standing still for long.’

So we walked on, all among the spring crocuses, and Seamus, pushing back his curly white hair as it blew over his forehead and from time to time stroking his short white beard, began.

Father Gillespie was already an old man when I first met him. He’d been sent to fill in for Father Cormigan, who was our parish priest before we got Father Donnelly. Father Cormigan had been ill over the winter, and he’d been told by the doctor to take a long break somewhere warm before taking up his duties again. I was just a young lad myself at this time, around thirteen, as I remember it.

When I met him Father Gillespie was sitting in the early spring sun-shine – warm enough for once – on the bench beside the bridge in the village street, and what attracted my attention was that he was reading a newspaper and seemed to be chuckling to himself. It was very unlike anything I’d ever seen Father Cormigan do, and I was interested enough to drift quietly over to him and glance unobtrusively over his shoulder.

He knew I was there, though, for all my stealth. But he didn’t seem to mind.

‘Hullo, young Seamus. Do you want to read my newspaper? Well, it’s good for a young lad like you to take an interest in reading.’

‘Yes, F-father,’ I stammered. I was taken aback to realise that he knew my name. But I found out later that Father Gillespie made a point of learning the names of all his parishioners, and, what’s more, of helping them when they were in need.

‘I’m just reading a very silly article about a woman writer of these romances, as they call them, a Miss Mercy Goodenough. The article says she’s been writing very successful romances for over ten years now, but no one knows who she is or anything about her. She ‘shuns publicity,’ it says. They’re suggesting that if anyone knows, they should write in to the newspaper and tell them. Offering a cash reward, too! The silly things people find interesting!’ He gave me a friendly grin. ‘So, sit down and tell me about yourself, Seamus.’

Nothing loath, I sat down on the bench and talked to him. Not too much about myself, for I didn't think he'd approve of some of my poaching activities. But there was plenty to talk about without that, for Father Gillespie, like me, loved the countryside and the plants and animals. And from then on we were the best of friends. I even started going to church sometimes to please him, though he never pushed me to.

It was several months after that when I noticed Father Gillespie walking along the riverbank under the leafy trees, muttering to himself, and occasionally making a note in a small pocket book. I was lying hidden in the long grass, looking up at a skylark, and he didn't see me at all. Suddenly he thrust the book back into his pocket, scrambled up the bank, and went hurrying away at a fierce pace. But as he climbed the bank, the notebook, sticking half out of his pocket, caught against the branch of the big chestnut tree which grew beside the river just there, and tumbled out, landing just beside me.

I sat up and caught it before it completed its journey and ended up in the river. Father Gillespie was almost out of sight by now. I decided I wouldn't try to catch up with him. Instead, I'd drop it in at his house later on.

The book was bent open, and I found that without meaning to I'd read some of the writing.

'My darling Josie, I love you so much. Didn't you realise that? Oh, I've tried to keep it secret. I thought no one need ever know. But I can't hide it any longer. You mean everything to me – I have to tell you so, no matter what comes of it!'

My mouth hung open. Father Gillespie writing stuff like that to a girl called Josie! I couldn't believe my eyes.

I was so gobsmacked that I sat on there for over an hour, wondering if there was anything I could do to help him. But I couldn't think of a thing. I knew that Father Gillespie wouldn't be allowed to marry this girl and still be a priest. It sounded as if that was what he wanted to do. So was he planning to give up the priesthood?

That would be a real pity, I thought, because he was the nicest priest I'd ever met. And anyway, wasn't he a bit old to be thinking of getting married? Even from my thirteen-year-old stance, I was pretty sure he was.

In the end I decided just to go along and give him back his notebook. And as for anything else, I'd just play it by ear. As you may have realised, I usually like to come up with some plan to help my friends, but this time I was really stumped. There seemed to be no happy solution possible.

I knocked reluctantly at the door of the presbytery where Father Gillespie was living until Father Cormigan came back to us. I was glad to see him open the door himself, instead of his grim faced housekeeper Mrs. Patterson.

'Come away in, Seamus!' he greeted me. 'Can you stay for a cup of tea? There's no one here to make it but me, but I'm not a bad hand at it.'

'Thanks, Father,' I said, following him into the kitchen. 'I really just came to give you back this. You dropped it by the river today.' I held out the notebook.

Father Gillespie's face was a picture – a horror picture. He turned white and panic showed in his eyes.

'Oh. Thank you, Seamus,' he managed after a full minute of silence. 'Em – did you read any of it?'

'Just a few words, Father. It was lying open, and I couldn't help seeing –'

'Oh, dear save us, I'm done for!' Father Gillespie moaned.

'Now, don't say that, Father!' I exclaimed. 'I'd never repeat it to anyone, don't you know that?'

Father Gillespie staggered over to a nearby chair and more or less collapsed onto it. 'You're a good boy, Seamus. I dread to think what would happen to me if the Bishop ever found out!'

I hated to see him so upset. 'Well, neither he nor anyone else will ever find out from me, I can promise you,' I said briskly, and was glad to see some colour returning to his cheeks. I lifted the kettle and filled it with water, then put it to boil on the cooker. 'A cup of tea will help you, Father.'

'A cup of tea would be good, Seamus. You're a good boy,' he repeated.

I sat down near him while we waited for the kettle to boil. 'But, Father,' I said gently, 'I think you're worrying too much about this. Isn't everyone going to know all about it if you marry this girl? And you'll have to give up being a priest anyway, if that's what you want to do, so the Bishop's opinion won't matter to you, will it?' I decided it wouldn't be very tactful to mention that maybe he was a bit old to be thinking of getting married and would be better off forgetting all about this Josie.

Father Gillespie stared at me with his mouth open, as if he didn't understand what I meant. Then, all of a sudden, he burst into a gigantic roar of laughter. There were tears streaming down his face and he was clutching his stomach in agony, bent over in the chair and looking as if he would never to able to stop. I stared at him stupidly, not knowing what to say.

Presently he wiped the tears of laughter from his eyes and sat up straight again. 'Och, Seamus, Seamus, you'll be the death of me! Did you think from what you read that I was in love with someone and thinking of getting married, at my age?'

I stared at him indignantly. If he wasn't planning to marry this girl, didn't that make it even worse? No wonder he was worried about what the Bishop would say!

'Wait and I'll show you,' Father Gillespie said through his remaining chuckles. He went across to the door and into the front room. Going to a locked cupboard, he opened it, took out several paperback volumes, and handed them to me.

'I keep these under lock and key,' he said. 'And usually I keep my current notebook locked up too, except when I'm using it. It was really careless of me to drop it today. I'll have to be more careful with it in future.'

I looked at the top book in the pile he given me. It said, *'Under Burning Skies'* and showed a picture of a man and a girl with their arms round each other on what was clearly meant to be a tropical island. The author's name beneath was Mercy Goodenough.

'Me,' said Father Gillespie, pointing to the name. 'I've been writing these romances for years. I enjoy it, and it brings in a bit of extra money above my stipend. Means I can help people who need it, sometimes. But if it ever got out that I was writing stuff like this –! I'd be the laughing stock of the parish. Probably be thrown out, and never get another position again! So you see why it has to be a secret, Seamus?'

I was impressed by Father Gillespie's cleverness, writing books, even romances, but I could see why he wouldn't want people to know, and him a priest. I still meant what I'd said about never giving him away, but I couldn't resist teasing him a little.

'Och, Father,' I said, 'and here was me thinking I could get that reward the newspaper was offering by telling them who Miss Mercy Goodenough is!'

For a moment Father Gillespie stared at me. Then his face relaxed. 'You young rogue, Seamus O'Hare! You had me going for a moment there!'

'You know you can trust me, Father,' I said. 'No one hears about your romances from me.'

And I kept my word from that day to this.

But the good Father went to meet his Lord a while ago now, so here I am telling his story to you. I know you don't know anyone who would remember Father Gillespie – I'm the only one, now. So it won't matter, after all these years, if you do repeat it!'

9 Daisy in the Country

There was a good country smell in the air as I put my head out of the door of my little cottage in the small Donegal village of Ardnakil – a mixture of the manure farmers were busily spreading on their fields, the freshly cut grass, and the scents of the blossoming flowers. The fresh green leaves were growing thicker on the trees, pale green larch mingling with the deeper green of the chestnut. Spring had arrived with a bound, and I was very happy to be here in Ardnakil for a few days break instead of working away at my busy city job.

It was far too good a day to stay indoors, and as soon as I'd washed up my breakfast dishes I wandered outside, strolling along the narrow lanes between the banks and hedges which were wearing their new spring dresses of creamy white hawthorn flowers and sweet smelling delicate bluebells. As I strolled on in the direction of the village, I felt that I was breathing in peace and happiness.

Across the middle of the wide village street the river streamed and bubbled in excitement as it forced its way under the bridge over rocks and boulders, in a green and white froth. I sat down for a few moments on the bench just beside the bridge, and was pleased to see my old friend Seamus O'Hare dander up, his hands in his pockets, his deplorable old hat pushed to the back of his head showing his white curls, and his disreputable old pipe in his mouth. As he saw me, Seamus altered his direction and came over to sit beside me, his brown, weather-beaten face creased into delighted wrinkles.

'Jamie, my boy! Great to see you!'

'You too, Seamus!'

I'd known Seamus since, as a boy, I came up to visit my grand-parents in the small whitewashed cottage they'd since left me, and he'd taught me everything I knew about the countryside, the birds, flowers, trees and animals.

'What a day, Seamus!' I said. 'I really love this place!'

'Ah, Jamie, you love coming to Ardnakil for a holiday, but I don't know if you would ever want to live here permanently.'

'Someday, Seamus, someday I might. But you're right, I need to stay in the city and work for a while yet. It's a real problem. I'm torn between the country and the town. When I'm here, I want to stay forever. But when I'm in the city, I love that, too.'

'I knew a girl who had the same problem,' Seamus said. 'Her name was Daisy. A lovely name, I've always thought. Did you know that it comes from Day's Eye, because each little daisy flower opens up in the morning and closes in the evening as if it were the day's own eyes?'

'So, is this a story, Seamus?'

'Well, I suppose it is, boy. I'll tell it to you, if you like.' Seamus leaned back on the wooden bench, puffed at his pipe, and began.

Daisy came from the city, but, like you, she had family here, her aunt Millie in fact, whom I knew well. She used to visit Millie from time to time, and Millie introduced us, so we became friends. I enjoyed Daisy's visits, and when she called in to see me, she would tell me what was happening in her life.

And after a while, I noticed how often her conversation veered towards young Michael Keenan, a local farmer. Michael was a fine, upstanding young man. He'd inherited the farm from his father, and he was making a good job of it. He was fair haired, brown eyed, and strong, his body well muscled, and his teeth gleaming white when he smiled, as he often did, for he had a happy, friendly nature and got on well with everyone. It was no wonder Daisy was fascinated by him.

'Michael loves the countryside,' Daisy told me wistfully. 'There's no way he'd want to move to the city to be with me. But I don't know if I'm really a country girl, Seamus. Mind you – ' Daisy smiled at me bewitchingly, pushing back her thick chestnut hair, her slate grey eyes shining in her lovely face – 'I think I might be willing to move here, just to be with him, if it came to that. I really like him, Seamus.'

'And I think he likes you, Daisy,' I told her. 'All you need to do is to get used to the country, show Michael you enjoy being here, right? I don't think that should be too hard.'

That same night, Michael Keenan dropped in to see me. It seems I've got a bit of a reputation as a local match maker, for it became clear quite soon that he had come looking for advice. He muttered and he mumbled, and then out with it.

'I really love her, Seamus,' he told me, 'but how can I expect her to live with me in the country, where there's so little to offer her, compared with the city where she lives now?'

'I wouldn't worry too much about that, Michael.' I told him. 'I think Daisy could grow to love the country if you gave her a half a chance.'

'Do you really think so?' Michael asked eagerly.

'I do, Michael,' I said. 'Here's a suggestion for you. Why don't you take her for a walk or two? Or introduce her to some of the cuter animals? New lambs, for instance. Or baby goats. She'd love them, and that would encourage her to love everything else about the country, I should think.'

And it occurred to me that I might suggest to Daisy that she'd maybe get to like the place if she went for a few walks on her own, and just let herself relax and enjoy the beauty of the fields and woods and flowers. I had a chat with her on the subject a day or so later.

'Go out and about, Daisy,' I told her. 'Let yourself have a chance to fall in love with the scents and sounds and colours, the birds singing their hearts out, the flowers and the plants bursting out in leaf and blossom and animals skipping and running about in the fields. This is the perfect time of year for it.'

'Well, I think I might, Seamus,' Daisy said. She sounded a bit hesitant, but I thought she was taking the idea seriously.

And sure enough, it was only a few days later that, as I strolled through the fields, I saw Daisy, dressed in a pretty blue frock with her name flower, the daisy, dotted over it in white with yellow centres, and with red strawberries and green wheat sprinkled among the flowers. She was walking slowly and rather carefully through one of the fields near me, tiptoeing cautiously over the rough grass, and making very sure to avoid the cowpats. She was clearly trying out the experience of walking in the country, and of practising being in the country fields. I thought she might have been better sticking to the lanes at first. The fields are always rougher and more difficult to walk on than they look from a distance. Still, I was glad she was giving it a go.

It wasn't clear to me just how much she was actually enjoying it – in fact, I thought after watching her for a while that maybe it wasn't such a good idea after all. As I watched her pulling her high-heeled shoes out of a muddy patch, and trying to avoid the cowpats, I couldn't help laughing. I hoped she wouldn't slip on one of the cowpats and go down – that would just about finish it! There was a sweet country smell of grass and wild roses in the air, but I didn't think Daisy was appreciating it too much from what I could see of her expression.

As I watched, I could see that a huge brown animal, horns projecting over its lowered forehead, eyes gleaming with excitement, was growing nearer to Daisy by the minute. Then Daisy looked up, and saw it. She froze.

From two fields away, I could hear Daisy's shriek. 'Help! Help me, some-one! There's a bull attacking me!'

I started to run towards her, then an idea occurred to me. A short while before, I'd passed Michael working in a nearby field, raking up the hay. So instead of heading straight for Daisy, I swerved towards the next field where I was pretty sure I would find Michael.

Sure enough, he was still there, busy as ever, putting his back into his task. For a minute he was too engrossed to see me, but when he heard me shouting he looked up with a start.

'Michael, Daisy's in the pasture, in big trouble! She's calling for help – she says a bull's attacking her – you'd better run!'

'In the pasture? But …!'

'Don't waste time, Michael my boy!' I ordered him severely. 'Daisy's very upset! She needs you!'

Without a second's more delay, Michael dropped his rake and went leaping across the field, jumped the stile, and headed for the pasture. By now he could hear Daisy's shrieks growing louder every minute as the huge brown animal came nearer.

'Daisy!' Michael called as he drew nearer to her. 'Just stand still, love! I'll look after you!'

Daisy, hearing his voice, turned round and, paying no attention to what he said, raced towards him, her arms reaching out to grasp him, as if he were her only hope of safety. The big brown animal lumbered after her.

Michael gathered Daisy into his arms and wasted some time kissing her very thoroughly. I watched them from the stile, waiting to see what would happen next.

Thrusting Daisy behind him at last, Michael strode forward.

'Back!' he ordered sternly, waving his arms. I wondered if he'd regretted dropping his rake. However, it was clear that he didn't need it. The animal halted in its tracks, then turning slowly began to move away.

'Oh, Michael,' Daisy cried, throwing her arms round him, 'how brave you are! You're wonderful!'

'Come on, love,' Michael said firmly. 'Let's get out of here!' Holding her closely, he half pushed half carried her to the edge of the field and out through the gate at the far end.

I was too far away to hear what was being said, but I could see that there was a lot more kissing going on.

I wondered if Daisy's frightening experience might have put her off the country altogether, but I needn't have worried. When she called in to see me the following afternoon, she couldn't stop talking about how marvellous Michael was.

'He's taking me into Millerstown tomorrow to buy a ring,' she confided shyly. 'And he says I needn't be frightened of anything in the country, because he'll look after me. We're going to be married after Michael has the hay all in, and we'll live at the farm, and Michael was showing me the baby lambs, and he says I can help to bring one up sometime when there's one that's lost its mother, by feeding it with a bottle! I think that'll be lovely!'

'So, everything's worked out well, then, Daisy?'

'Oh, yes, it certainly has, Seamus. Michael says I must be careful where I go for walks. I should stick to the lanes if he isn't with me. I was very silly going into that field with the bull, wasn't I?'

'Well, it's a fact that you need to check what sort of animal might be in a field before you go for a walk through it, Daisy,' was all I said.

Later that evening Michael also called round.

'So, you've persuaded Daisy to settle down with you in the country, in spite of everything, Michael?' I asked him.

'Yes.' Michael looked a bit shamefaced. 'She seems to think I'm some sort of hero, chasing off a bull and rescuing her. Anyway, the main thing is, she's decided that the country life with all its risks will be fine as long as she's with me, and she says she'll listen to any advice I give her and she won't go anywhere on her own unless I tell her it's safe.'

'Well, isn't that great, boy?' I said. 'That sounds like the recipe for a happy life – maybe. As long as it lasts. But I tell you something, Michael, if I were you I'd move that animal into a different field, my boy, before Daisy sees it again.'

Michael looked at me, and he saw that I knew the truth. He couldn't help smiling. 'Well, you could be right there, Seamus,' he grinned.

'Ten to one if it's somewhere else Daisy will never recognise it,' I said. 'But it would be a real pity, so it would, if she took a better look at it another time, and if she stopped thinking you're such a hero as all that, when she notices that your dangerous bull has udders!'

10 Seamus and the Family Tree

Summer was in full flow, warm sunny days interspersed with rain. I'd been working too hard for months. It was time I took a break from the stifling heat of the big city. As always my thoughts turned to the little Donegal village of Ardnakil, and the small whitewashed cottage my grandparents left me. In Ardnakil, with its fresh river running through the centre, its open fields and shady trees, I could always find peace.

I threw some clothes into a bag, and set off. Soon I was surrounded by the green and beautiful fields and hills and flowers of my heart's desire.

I took my bag into the cottage, relaxed with my feet up and a cup of tea, then went out in search of my old friend Seamus O'Hare.

I've known Seamus since I was a boy, staying with my grandparents. Already an established poacher, he taught me everything I know about country flowers and animals, and even showed me how to tickle a trout. Now, as an adult, it's been my pleasure to keep up the friendship.

I found him in one of his favourite spots, under the trees on the river-bank a few miles from the village, lying back watching the flight of a lark above him and listening to its sweet song.

'Hello, Jamie my boy,' he greeted me, sitting up. 'Come and join me.' His wrinkled old face was brown as ever from sun and wind, his curly hair white beneath his battered old cap, and his bright eyes twinkled at me beneath bushy white eyebrows. His disreputable old pipe stuck out of his mouth, surrounded by his curly white beard.

'It's good to see you, Seamus,' I said, sitting down beside him with a sigh of pleasure. 'How are things with you?'

'Oh, things are good with me. They always are. But how about yourself, Jamie?'

'Better, now I'm here, Seamus. It's been a busy time in work. And to make matters worse, I've been tied up with some family commitments. My cousin Kathleen from America is over, and she's wanting my help to track down all our great, great grandparents and such. I've never met her before. She's a lot older than me, but still very fit and spry, and she tells me she thought she'd better come over now, while she still has her health.

Looking up your family tree means a lot of running around different churches arranging to see their registers of family weddings and christenings. And a lot of crawling about graveyards trying to make out the inscriptions on old headstones. She's headed off down Tipperary direction to look up a side branch, and I thought I'd take the opportunity to get offside for a while.'

'It's a mystery to me why folks have got so interested in that sort of thing these days,' Seamus said comfortably, puffing at his pipe. 'I never had any family tree to speak off, and just look at me!' We both laughed, and then Seamus said, 'It used to be no one would worry about all that unless there was an inheritance involved. Though, come to think of it, there was young Eileen O'Grady, who spent a great deal of time trying to trace her ancestors with no thought of an inheritance.'

'And are you going to tell me Eileen's story, Seamus?' I asked, lying back against the grassy bank.

'Well, I will if you like, Jamie.' Seamus lay back in turn, puffed at his pipe, and began.

I met Eileen when she was not much older than me, about fifteen to my thirteen. She was brought up in an orphanage and when she was old enough they got her a job at Mrs Dolan's guesthouse as a maid of all work. Mrs Dolan was a kind enough body, but Eileen worked long hard hours every day.

I had gone into the churchyard for no particular reason one evening in the summer. It was still light, and as I perched myself on one of the raised slabs of granite to have a think I saw someone bent down, peering at one of the headstones.

My curiosity aroused, I went over to her, and she looked up at me with a friendly smile. She had a sweet little face with rosy cheeks and dimples, and her hair was an unusual shade of red gold, curling round her ears. 'Hello,' she said. 'I can't make out this name – do you think it might be O'Grady?'

I bent down to have a closer look at the weathered carving, but it didn't look like O'Grady to me. 'I think it's Grafton,' I said, and saw her smile fade, to be replaced by a look of disappointment. 'Why, did you want it to be O'Grady?'

'Well, that's my own name,' she explained. 'Eileen O'Grady. I'm trying to find some of my family.'

'I'm Seamus O'Hare.'

She seemed a nice girl. I decided to give her a hand, and until the sun set a few hours later we covered that churchyard thoroughly. But we saw no sign of any O'Gradys.

'I suppose they may not come from round here,' said Eileen at last with a sigh, which she tried to cover with a smile. 'It was just a chance.'

'Don't you know where your family come from?' I asked her.

'No. You see, Seamus, I was brought up in the parish orphanage, and no one there knows anything about me. I was left on the doorstep when I was only a week or so old. But the parish church seemed a good place to start if I was going to find any family of my own.'

I couldn't help wondering if a family who'd left you on an orphanage door-step would be worth finding. But I didn't want to discourage her.

'So how do you know that your family is called O'Grady?' I asked.

'Oh, that's the nice part of the story!' Eileen said eagerly. 'When I was leaving the orphanage to go to Mrs Dolan's, Matron called me in for a fare-well chat, and gave me something I'd had as a baby – this little silver bracelet.' She produced a tiny bracelet from her pocket and showed it to me. 'It has Eileen O'Grady engraved on it, so that was how they knew my name. It was round my wrist. I couldn't wear it now, it would be much too small, but I'll always keep it, whether I find my family or not. Someone must have cared about me, to give me this bracelet.'

I could see the tears starting in her eyes, and hurried to move the discussion on. 'Why not make an appointment with Father Gillespie and ask him if he knows any O'Gradys?' I suggested. 'He would look up the register for you, anyway. He's a very kind man.'

Eileen brightened up. 'That's a great idea, Seamus!' she exclaimed. 'I suppose it's a bit late to worry him now, but I'll call tomorrow evening as soon as I finish at Mrs Dolan's. I don't suppose – ' she hesitated – 'I don't suppose you'd come with me?'

'Of course I will, Eileen,' I promised her.

So the next evening we met up at Father Gillespie's house and knocked at the door. The grim-faced housekeeper, Mrs Patterson, opened it presently, and seemed to be in two minds about letting us in, but Father Gillespie must have heard the voices, for he came bustling out from his study and greeted us with the utmost friendliness. 'Come away in, there, Seamus. And who's your pretty little friend?'

'This is Eileen O'Grady, Father,' I said. 'Eileen's looking for a bit of help, trying to track down her family tree. I thought maybe you could look up the parish registers for her?'

'I'd be happy to do that, Eileen,' said Father Gillespie. 'But I have to warn you that O'Grady isn't a name I've come across around here. Still, no harm in looking!'

He called to Mrs Patterson to bring some tea and scones, and led the way into his study where the parish records were stowed in a locked strongbox.

As he opened the box with a huge iron key, Father Gillespie asked Eileen a few questions, and soon had the story out of her of how she'd been left at the Orphanage.

'A sad story, my child. People had some very wrong ideas at that time. They were ashamed to own a child born out of wedlock, instead of seeing that every child is a blessing from the Lord, and so they tried to pretend the child didn't exist or was nothing to do with them. A sad thing.'

Father Gillespie was assiduous in searching the thick registers, but by the time we'd finished our tea and eaten all the scones, he had still found no sign of a family called O'Grady. Every now and then he would give Eileen a friendly smile, and it seemed to me that he was studying her face closely as he did so.

Finally, he sat back in his chair, sighed, and closing the last volume of the register said, 'Do you know, I don't think we're getting anywhere with this. But I'm an old fool, or I've have told you right at the start that the place for you to look would be in the Library in Millerstown. I'm sure Mrs Dolan would give you an afternoon off to go there. Tell her it would be a real favour to me if she would. And I daresay young Seamus here would be happy to go with you for company.'

'Are some of the records kept there, Father?' I asked him.

'The reference books are, Seamus. You just take Eileen along and see.'

Mrs Dolan was happy to oblige her parish priest, so a few days later Eileen and I caught the bus to Millerstown and made our way to the library. Eileen was a bit reluctant to take the lead, so I went up to the desk where the librarian, a woman in her mid thirties with reddish hair, was sitting writing in a ledger. I coughed to draw her attention, and she looked up.

'Yes? Can I help you?'

I beckoned Eileen over from where she was hovering shyly by the door. 'It's really my friend Eileen O'Grady here who'd like some help,' I began, but stopped abruptly. The librarian had jumped to her feet and was standing swaying beside her desk, her hands clasped to her heart, her eyes fixed on Eileen's face.

'Eileen O'Grady! It can't be!' she said under her breath, so that I could only just hear her. Then she slid to the ground in a dead faint.

'Help!' I called, springing round to reach her and to support her as she fell. A man came running across from a desk further away, and called imperatively to someone else to fetch a glass of water. A girl arrived with a brimming glass and they propped up the white faced librarian. In a few more moments she had opened her eyes, and they persuaded her to take a sip.

'Eileen? Where is she?' the woman asked faintly.

'She's here,' I said, pushing Eileen forward. 'Do you know her?'

'Know her? Eileen's my sister! But she's dead!'

'Maybe we could go somewhere to talk privately?' I suggested. Presently we found ourselves in a little room off the main library, and there I told Eileen's story to the librarian, and got Eileen to show her the bracelet.

'My name is O'Grady – Sinead O'Grady,' she said, tears running down her face. 'My sister Eileen had a baby when she was fifteen. Michael and Eileen weren't married, they were both too young, and he was killed in a traffic accident before the baby was born. Eileen died in a nursing home giving birth. I only saw the baby once, in the nursing home, and I put that bracelet I'd bought her on her wrist. My father told me the baby had died a week later. He must have lied – trying to cover up the shame. He was such a respect-able man. But I wouldn't have thought he could be so hard. Eileen, Eileen, you're the picture of your mother. You're just the age that I remember her at.' And she threw her arms round Eileen and hugged and kissed her.

Well, we hadn't found any records at the library, but we'd found something even better. Sinead O'Grady insisted that Eileen should come to live with her and go back to school until she was qualified for a better job than scrubbing in a guesthouse, and Eileen was only too delighted.

As for me, I'd been looking from Sinead to Eileen, and seeing the resemblance staring out at me. I knew now why Father Gillespie had sent us here. The cunning old man had been to the library often enough to remember what the librarian looked like, and he'd been pretty sure that if Eileen turned up there, she'd have no problem in finding at least one member of her family!

11 Paddy and the Snake

I looked up doubtfully at the hazy sky and wondered what sort of day it was going to be. I had only a few days' holiday to spend at the little white-washed cottage I'd inherited from my grandparents in the small Donegal village of Ardnakil, and I was hoping that the weather, which had been very pleasant up until now, wasn't going to break. It was late autumn, but the last few weeks had been more like summer.

Deciding to chance it, I strolled out as I was, and wandered through the fields and lanes. Presently I heard a melodious whistling and realised with pleasure that it must be my old friend Seamus O'Hare. I'd known Seamus since my childhood when I came up to visit my grandparents, and Seamus had taught me country lore, how to tell a chaffinch from a wagtail and a larch tree from a beech. I walked on and rounded a corner of the lane. There he was, strolling along, his disreputable old pipe in one hand and his old hat crammed down on his white curly hair.

'Jamie!' he exclaimed. 'I'm glad to see you, boy! Are you going my way?'

'I can go whichever way you like, Seamus,' I said obligingly, falling into step beside him. 'I'm just out to enjoy a walk with no special object in view.'

'Hasn't the weather been perfect?' Seamus asked, his engaging smile lighting up his wrinkled, weather beaten old face. 'Especially for so late in the year, when summer's well over. Sure, it would lift your heart up just to see the sun so bright every day.'

And sure enough, the sun had come beaming out from behind the hazy clouds just as we met up, to bring a heartful of happiness with it. We walked on in contentment and presently we came in sight of the river, flowing smoothly along, its waters gleaming with silver ripples in the light of the sunshine.

'It's the sort of day,' Seamus said, puffing his pipe contentedly, 'when you want to take your girl by the hand and stroll off into the distance, sit down on the grass beneath a tree and share a picnic while you chat.'

I gave him a quizzical look. 'And is that what you used to do on days like these, Seamus?' I asked him, smiling.

‘Ah, well, once in a while and a long time ago, Jamie,’ he answered me, smiling in his turn. ‘I’ve some happy memories of that sort of thing. But my friend Paddy Doyle, now, his experience was different.’

‘And are you going to tell me about it, Seamus?’

‘Let’s sit down, ourselves, under this tree by the side of the river, Jamie, and I’ll do that.’

And when we were comfortably seated on the grassy bank beneath a flourishing ash tree which dropped the occasional leaf on our heads, Seamus began his story.

Paddy was a bit of a joker. He was a big, happy-go-lucky sort of a fella, and most people liked him – except some who had no sense of humour and weren’t very pleased with the tricks he played on them. At the time I’m speaking of, Paddy was going out with a bright young red haired girl by the name of Maureen O’Flynn.

Maureen was a lovely lass and could have had her pick of all the local fellas, but it seemed as if her heart was set on Paddy. And as for Paddy himself, he wasn’t without his own admirers, being a fine upstanding young man with fair curly hair and a beaming smile. But there was no one but Maureen for him.

It was a warm, sunny, autumn day, much like today, when Paddy and Maureen went for a stroll and a picnic along the river banks, and at first all went, as the poet says, ‘as merrily as a wedding bell.’ In fact, as Maureen sat leaning her cheek against Paddy’s broad shoulder, she was thinking of wedding bells herself, and wondering if Paddy would choose this opportunity to ask her to name the day. But, alas, Paddy had other thoughts in his mind right then.

‘Isn’t this lovely, Paddy dear?’ sighed Maureen.

‘Indeed it is, Maureen,’ Paddy replied. Then, seizing his chance as a leaf floated down from the huge chestnut tree above them and touched Maureen gently on her right cheek, he exclaimed, ‘Oh! For dear sakes, Maureen, look out! It’s a snake!’

And at the same moment he threw down a withered branch of a tree, which he’d picked up and hidden behind his back a few moments before they sat down, right at Maureen’s feet.

‘Ow!’ shouted Maureen, leaping up and shrieking loud enough to be heard in Millerstown. ‘Paddy, Paddy, save me!’

Then as she tried to escape from the 'snake' she tripped over Paddy's feet, which I have to admit were on the outsize side, and went plunging and shouting over the edge of the river bank and straight into the water.

Well, Paddy's joke had gone off even better than he had hoped, and he stood on the bank and roared with laughter as Maureen, dripping wet and furious, stood up in the water, which at that point was shallow enough to be no danger, and came only to her knees.

'Maureen, Maureen, you'll be the death of me!' exclaimed Paddy. 'Don't you know that the holy Saint Patrick threw all the snakes out of our blessed Ireland over fifteen hundred years ago?' And he brandished the piece of wood he'd used to trick Maureen.

But Maureen, whose best clothes and new sandals were, she thought, probably ruined, wasn't in any mood to laugh.

Ignoring Paddy's outstretched hand, she scrambled out of the river by herself, and stalked off in the direction of home and dry clothes, saying only, as she left, 'Don't you ever dare to speak to me again, Paddy Doyle! You're a disgrace to Irish manhood!'

Paddy's jaw dropped. He stood, gazing after her, unable to believe his ears. Sure, it had been a very funny joke, hadn't it? Ach, Maureen would get over it in a short while and be ready to laugh along with him.

But the days went past, and Maureen showed no sign of getting over it. When she and Paddy accidentally met in the village street she swept past him with her nose in the air, leaving poor Paddy gaping after her helplessly.

In the end, he did what so many of my young friends have done, he came to me for help. 'What am I going to do, Seamus?' he asked when he had told me the story. 'I still love her, even if she has no sense of humour. What am I going to do?'

But for once I was at a loss. 'Paddy, you've dug yourself a hole and fallen in,' I told him. 'As far as I can see, you can only wait for Time the Great Healer to soften Maureen's heart towards you.'

But this was small consolation for Paddy, who like all youngsters had no desire to wait for anything.

But as it happened, only the next night young Maureen O'Flynn also called at my cottage.

'Seamus, please help me!' she begged. And then the same story came tumbling out, but from Maureen's angle, and I heard all about how she'd been full of romantic thoughts and expecting Paddy to speak when he spoiled everything with his silly joke. 'I can't go through my life, Seamus, having everything spoilt by Paddy playing a silly trick at the most romantic moments,' she said, with the tears starting up in her eyes. 'Can't you help me?'

I sat gazing into the turf fire and smelling the aroma of the smoking turf, and then I said, 'You know what, Maureen, I think I might have an idea. Now, listen.'

And Maureen listened, and then she smiled, and then she laughed.

A few days later Paddy Doyle was called to the door of his cottage by the rap of the postman.

'Parcel for you, Paddy,' wee Andy Devlin, the postman, said. 'Sign here.'

Paddy, who wasn't expecting anything, signed, and then stood turning the parcel round in his hands for a few moments before opening it. His face brightened suddenly as he saw the sender's name on the back in large bold printing. Maureen O'Flynn, 42 Millpond Lane, Ardnakil. Was Maureen wanting to make it up, then, that she was sending him a present? Had she realised that his joke had been both funny and harmless? He hadn't expected her to fall into the river, after all!

He tore the parcel open eagerly, peeling off the brown paper. Inside were more wrappings, newspaper this time. Tearing them off, Paddy came to a box sealed with a large amount of sellotape. He ran for a knife and cut through the worst of it. Finally he was able to open the box, and found that it was full of cotton wool.

Eagerly Paddy pulled off the cotton wool. There, staring up at him, was an enormous spider, black and ominous looking, with a notice beside it – 'Tarantula – beware! Dangerous!'

With a howl, Paddy hurled the box from him and raced out of his cottage.

He had run about a hundred yards down the road when Maureen O'Flynn stepped out from the hedge into his way and said sweetly, 'Why, Paddy, don't you know there are no tarantulas in Ireland?'

Paddy skidded to a halt. His visual memory of the spider came flooding back. Suddenly he realised that the insect which had frightened him so much has been an imitation, made of rubber, and nothing else.

I'll say this for Paddy, he could take a joke as well as play one. It only took him a minute to recover. 'Maureen, Maureen, you'll be the death of me!' he said, putting his arms round her. 'I knew you had a great sense of humour all along!'

'Yes, well, that's all right, Paddy Doyle,' said Maureen severely – not making any attempt to wriggle out of his arms, however. 'But maybe now you understand what it's like to be on the receiving end of one of your funny jokes. Not too great, is it?'

And Paddy had to admit that it wasn't. 'Maureen, you had me scared out of my wits!' he admitted generously. 'I hadn't time to think how unlikely it would be to find a tarantula in Ireland, any more than you had time to think about St. Patrick driving out the snakes. I'm sorry, love – I shouldn't have done it. And I certainly never expected you to fall into the river!'

'Yes, well, that'll be enough about that, Paddy,' said Maureen, whose dignity had suffered as much as her clothes from her unexpected bathe. 'We'll not discuss that any more, if you don't mind. All I want from you, Paddy Doyle, is a promise that you'll never play a trick like that on me again. I'm not going to spend the rest of my life in fear that you've got something up your sleeve for me every time I open a present.'

Paddy only heard one thing. 'Spend the rest of your life!' he exclaimed joyously. 'Maureen, do you mean it? Will you?'

'Only if I have your promise, Paddy.'

'Ach, Maureen, of course you have it,' Paddy murmured as he put him arms round her more tightly and kissed her.

And certainly the ring he bought her the next day was no joke, for it cost Paddy most of his savings, and it was as well he had his parents house, left to him some years ago, to take Maureen to. He only asked for one thing.

'Maureen,' he said anxiously, 'Can I play tricks on other people as long as I don't play any on you?'

'Sure you can, Paddy!' Maureen said generously. 'And I tell you what, I'll make a promise, too. I won't play any tricks on you, as long as I can play them on other people. For, Paddy, just as you saw how awful it was to be on the receiving end, I saw for myself how much fun it was to be the one playing the tricks, and I don't think I'm planning to stop now!'

And she was as good as her word. Neither Paddy nor Maureen played any tricks on each other, but they played plenty on other people, so that the name of Doyle became famous the length and breadth of the county for joking. Especially when Maureen's name was Doyle as well as Paddy's – which it became in a very short time afterwards.

12 Bridie's Christmas Holiday

I usually manage to get up to Donegal around Christmas, to the little white washed cottage in Ardakil my grandparents left me. And while I'm there I like to catch up with my friend old Seamus O'Hare.

It was bitterly cold. Instead of going for a walk, I hurried down to the village and put my head round the door of the *Golden Pheasant,* our local pub. Sure enough, there was Seamus, sitting up at the bar with a pint of the black stuff, his disreputable old pipe in one hand. Not lit, of course, with the new laws – I suppose he held it from habit. When he saw me, he smiled, his brown, weather beaten face wrinkling with pleasure.

'Not going outside for a smoke, Seamus?' I asked, grinning, as I ordered a pint of my own.

'Not in this weather, boy! To think that these days I can't have a smoke indoors with my pint! Things change, don't they? And not always for the better.'

'You're right there, Seamus,' I agreed.

'Still there have been good changes as well as bad in my lifetime,' Seamus added thoughtfully. 'People are treated better, mostly. When I think of wee Bridie Magee and how her employers treated her, when I was a youngster!'

'Is it a story, Seamus?' I asked hopefully.

'I suppose it could be, Jamie. Let's move over to the corner table, and I'll tell you about Bridie.' When we were settled in the corner of the bar, Seamus began.

Bridie Magee had worked for the Hamiltons for several years, since she left the orphanage at the age of sixteen. She did some housework for them, but her main job was to look after their two children, Mark and Debbie, and spoilt brats they were.

They made Bridie's life a misery, for she wasn't allowed to punish them, and when she reported any particularly bad behaviour to their parents, such as the time they tripped her up and sent her flying down the stairs, or when they 'accidentally' spilt ink all over her clean apron, it would be shrugged off with, 'Och, they're high spirited youngsters. They mean no harm.' Bridie would have left if she had had any idea where to go, but work wasn't so easy to come by in those days.

Bridie had a good friend, Johnny Lynch, who came round to see her whenever he could, and who constantly advised her to leave. Bridie wasn't supposed to have friends visiting her, but Johnny usually managed to slip in quietly through the kitchen garden to meet her. He was a great help to her with the children, for Johnny was a tall, strong youngster, four years older than Bridie, and Mark and Debbie were in awe of him. So far they hadn't mentioned his presence to their parents, to Bridie's relief. She knew that as soon as the Hamiltons found out, she would be forbidden to have Johnny round ever again.

But the day came when Mark tried to push Bridie into the lily pond, and Johnny, very angry, seized him and administered a hard slap on the seat of his trousers. Mark burst into unnecessary tears, more from fear than from any slight pain, and went roaring off to his mother, who immediately rushed to the scene of the crime. Johnny, unwilling to leave Bridie to deal with Lesley Hamilton by herself, stood his ground and attempted to explain what Mark had been doing, but Mrs Hamilton wasn't listening, and as Bridie had expected, Johnny was ordered to leave and forbidden ever to come back.

Now, I'd known Johnny for a good many years. He and I were much of an age, and we'd often gone fishing together. So it was natural that the next time we met up, Johnny poured out his troubles to me.

Then things got even worse.

It was nearly Christmas time. Bridie was due a holiday, and Johnny was expecting to see her. But this year, the Hamiltons had other plans. They had decided on a winter skiing holiday in Switzerland, and they had no intention of being hampered by their children while away. So Lesley Hamilton called Bridie into the drawing room one day and very graciously told her that they had booked a little holiday for her, at the time they themselves would be abroad.

'A delightful country inn, my dear,' she said. 'A farmhouse which takes paying guests. Good country food and lots of animals to amuse the children. Of course, I knew you'd want to have Mark and Debbie with you, so I've booked them in as well. No, no, don't thank me – you'd done so much for us, it's the least we can do in return. Just enjoy your holiday, that will be thanks enough.'

Bridie was at a loss for words. Did Mrs Hamilton really think it would be a holiday for her if she still had to look after Mark and Debbie? Bridie found it hard to believe.

That night she wrote a doleful little note to Johnny, explaining that she wouldn't be able to spend Christmas with him after all, because she would be away. Lesley Hamilton hadn't yet told her exactly where, so she wasn't able to give Johnny the address.

I came upon Johnny the next day, leaning over the bridge in Ardnakil, looking miserable. 'Here, Seamus, what d'ye think of that?' he said, handing Bridie's note to me.

I read it quickly. 'She seems pretty upset.'

'So she does. And so am I, Seamus. We were both looking forward to being able to see each other during her holiday. Now I don't even know where she's going to be!'

'Maybe I could find that out for you, Johnny,' I said slowly. 'And if you knew, would you plan to go there and meet up with her?'

'Would I? You bet I would, Seamus!'

'Well, be here tomorrow and I'll have news for you,' I said. 'Meanwhile, time you took steps to get your wee girl out of that job, Johnny boy!'

My idea was quite simple. I was very friendly, at that time, with the girl who ran the small village post office and telephone exchange. As soon as I left Johnny I headed there to see her. She was a pretty young lass, but a year or so afterwards she married and moved away, before I could decide if I wanted to spend the rest of my life with her. That's how it goes, you see, if you don't make up your mind in time.

'Top of the morning to you, Molly my dear,' I greeted her. 'You're looking extra pretty today!' And after a bit of banter back and forth, I got down to it. 'You see all the post here, Molly,' I began. 'You'll have seen letters from the Hamiltons booking their Christmas holidays?'

'Aye, right, holidays is the word!' Molly exclaimed. 'Two places, they've booked. I heard her ringing up about it on the switchboard, and then I saw the letters. A hotel in Switzerland for a fortnight, no less. And two weeks in a farmhouse away near Letterkenny. I heard her ringing up a friend to ask her to recommend somewhere cheap. The friend said this wasn't much of a place but the rates were as cheap as you'd get.'

'And did you notice the address, Molly my dear?'

'I did that, Seamus. It's *The Two Trees*, Dunkelly.'

I made a careful note of the address and next morning I passed it on to Johnny, who was delighted. He told me afterwards that he set off that same day by train and bus, across country, to get to the place.

It was late by the time he got there and he couldn't see much in the dark. The place was shut up and there were no lights. In the end he decided to put up in Letterkenny for the night and go out to *The Two Trees* again the following day.

When he got there, he was horrified at the broken down, shabby appearance of the farmhouse. An old, dilapidated building, it stood by itself, miles from the nearest houses, surrounded by neglected fields full of weeds. The only animals in sight were a couple of donkeys grazing forlornly in one of the fields. Johnny strode firmly up to the front door. The bell was broken. He seized the door knocker and thumped the flaking paint of the old wooden door. No one answered. Johnny called out in his most powerful roar, 'Bridie! Are you there?'

He listened hard, and heard a patter of flying feet. A moment later the door burst open, and Bridie came hurtling out into his arms.

'Oh, Johnny! How did you know I was here? It's so lovely to see you!'

Johnny held on to her and kissed her warmly. But after a few minutes, Bridie broke away and began to cry. 'Johnny, I'm in such trouble! I've lost the children!'

'Hush, darlin', hush now,' said Johnny, patting her arm.

'Johnny, I took them out for a walk this morning, because there's nothing else for them to do here, and they ran away from me! I don't know where they went – and anything might have happened to them – especially in this bitter cold!'

'Bitter cold is right,' agreed Johnny. 'I think it's starting to snow. Best come inside before we both freeze to death, girl.' He led her through the doorway, but was immediately struck by the fact that it was, if anything, even colder indoors than out. 'Dear sakes, what sort of a place is this for you to be staying, sweetheart?' he exclaimed.

'Oh, Johnny, it's a dreadful place,' Bridie shuddered. 'So cold, and the meals badly cooked and hardly enough to feed a bird! But never mind all that! What am I going to do about the children?'

'Do they have any money?' Johnny asked.

'Oh, yes, their parents always give them lots of pocket money. They have plenty.'

'Then my guess is that they've gone into Letterkenny to get the train back to Ardnakil, Bridie. And I think you and I had better do the same. Now, go and pack your things, for I'm not letting you stay here a moment longer.' And he sent her straight up to her room to pack.

While he was waiting an elderly woman came out from the back of the farmhouse to ask what he was doing there. Johnny soon sent her about her business. 'Let her go if she likes,' the woman said shrilly, 'but you needn't think you're getting any money back!'

'It's not my money, granny,' Johnny said cheerfully, 'so I can't say I'm worried.'

By the time Bridie came down with her suitcase, the woman had blustered herself away into the kitchen again.

Bridie still looked worried. 'Johnny, suppose the children come back here and find I've gone?' she asked anxiously.

'We'll leave a message for them, Bridie. But it's not likely. Anyone with the money to get away from here would be bound to go. We'll maybe catch up with them at the railway station. They'll not get a train before two o'clock – I know, because I checked the timetable yesterday. But if they aren't there, we'll report it to the Gardai.'

They got a lift on a passing cart which was going to Letterkenny, and went straight to the station. There, Johnny made Bridie wait out of the cold in the railway cafe with a warm cup of tea, while he searched for Mark and Debbie.

There was a sound of sobbing coming from the waiting room. Johnny went in. Debbie was crouched on one of the benches with her head buried in her arms, while Mark patted her in a brotherly fashion, his face showing dismay. He was clearly at a loss to know what to do. Johnny could see that both children realised they had made a big mistake. When they looked up and saw Johnny, joy spread over their faces.

'Well, that was a daft thing to do, wasn't it?' Johnny said cheerfully. 'Fancy getting yourselves lost at Christmas time! You might have missed your presents! Don't cry, Debbie. Come on and we'll get you both some hot soup. And after that we're going home to Ardnakil!'

Johnny didn't pull his punches when he phoned the Hamiltons that evening to tell them what he thought of their holiday farmhouse, and how badly they'd treated not only Bridie but their own children. They must have been ashamed, because they came rushing home from Switzerland to look after Mark and Debbie themselves over Christmas.

As for Bridie, Johnny refused to let her stay there once the Hamiltons were back. Instead, he whisked her away to his own parents, just until he could arrange for them to get married. 'No arguments, Bridie darlin',' he said. 'I should have done this long ago.' And Bridie was only too happy to agree.

You see, Johnny was a man who could make his mind up and be sure not to miss what he really wanted. He wasn't as foolish as me!

About the author

Gerry McCullough has been writing poems and stories since childhood. Brought up in north Belfast, she graduated in English and Philosophy from Queen's University, Belfast, then went on to gain an MA in English.

She lives in Northern Ireland, just outside Belfast,, has four grown up children and is married to author, media producer and broadcaster, Raymond McCullough, with whom she co-edited the Irish magazine, *Bread*, (originally published by *Kingdom Come Trust*), from 1990-96. In 1995 they also published a non-fiction book called, *Ireland – now the good news!*

Over the past few years Gerry has had around eighty short stories published in UK, Irish and American magazines, anthologies and annuals – as well as broadcast on BBC Radio Ulster – plus poems and articles published in several Northern Ireland and UK magazines. She has also read from her novels, poems and short stories at many Irish literary events.

Gerry won the *Cúirt International Literary Award* for 2005 (Galway); was shortlisted for the 2008 *Brian Moore Award* (Belfast); shortlisted for the 2009 *Cúirt Award*; commended in the 2009 *Seán O'Faolain Short Story Competition*, (Cork) and shortlisted in the 2015 *Harmony House Poetry Competition*, Downpatrick. In 2016 she also won the *Bangor Poetry Award* for her poem, *Summer Passing*.

Belfast Girls, her first full-length Irish novel, was first published (by *Night Publishing*, UK) in November 2010 (re-issued July 2012 by *Precious Oil). Danger Danger* was published by *Precious Oil Publications* in October 2011; followed by *The Seanachie: Tales of Old Seamus* in January 2012 (a first collection of humorous Irish short stories, previously published in a weekly Irish magazine); *Angel in Flight* (the first Angel Murphy thriller) in June 2012; *Lady Molly and the Snapper* – a young adult novel time travel adventure set in Dublin (August 2012); *Angel in Belfast* (the 2nd Angel Murphy thriller) in June 2013; *Johnny McClintock's War* in August 2014, *The Seanachie 2:*

Norah on the Beach in September 2014; *Hel's Heroes* in June 2015; *Dreams, Visions, Nightmares* (a collection of eight literary and award-winning Irish short stories), in January 2016; *Not the End of the World* (a comic, futuristic fantasy novel) in February 2016. *The Seanachie 3: Seamus and the Shell and other stories* in August 2016; *Angel in Paradise* (the 3rd Angel Murphy thriller) in January 2017; *Hel's Heroes 2: Christie and the Pirate* (2nd in the series) was released in March 2019. *The Seanachie 4: Paddy and the Snake and other stories* is Gerry's 15th release.

Belfast Girls

The story of three girls – Sheila, Phil and Mary – growing up into the new emerging post-conflict Belfast of money, drugs, high fashion and crime; and of their lives and loves.

Sheila, a supermodel, is kidnapped.

Phil is sent to prison.

Mary, surviving a drug overdose, has a spiritual awakening.

It is also the story of the men who matter to them –

John Branagh, former candidate for the priesthood, a modern Darcy, someone to love or hate. Will he and Sheila ever get together?

Davy Hagan, drug dealer, 'mad, bad and dangerous to know'. Is Phil also mad to have anything to do with him?

Although from different religious backgrounds, starting off as childhood friends, the girls manage to hold on to that friendship in spite of everything.

A book about contemporary Ireland and modern life. A book which both men and women can enjoy – thriller, romance, comedy, drama – and much more …

"fascinating ... original ... multilayered ...

expertly travels from one genre to the next"

Kellie Chambers, Ulster Tatler *(Book of the Month)*

"romance at the core ... enriched with breathtaking action, mystery, suspense and some tear-jerking moments of tragedy.

Sheila M. Belshaw*, author*

"What starts out as a crime thriller quickly evolves into a literary festival beyond the boundary of genres"

PD Allen*, author*

"a masterclass, and a vivid dissection of the human condition in all of its inglorious foibles"

WeeScottishLassie

Read the first chapter of **Belfast Girls**:

Belfast Girls

Gerry McCullough

Published by

Chapter One

Jan 21, 2007

The street lights of Belfast glistened on the dark pavements where, even now, with the troubles officially over, few people cared to walk alone at night. John Branagh drove slowly, carefully, through the icy streets.

In the distance, he could see the lights of the Magnifico Hotel, a bright contrasting centre of noise, warmth and colour.

He felt again the excitement of the news he'd heard today.

Hey, he'd actually made the grade at last – full-time reporter for BBC TV, right there on the local news programme, not just a trainee, any longer. Unbelievable.

The back end shifted a little as he turned a corner. He gripped the wheel tighter and slowed down even more. There was black ice on the roads tonight. Gotta be careful.

So, he needed to work hard, show them he was keen. This interview, now, in this hotel? This guy Speers? If it turned out good enough, maybe he could go back to Fat Barney and twist his arm, get him to commission it for local TV, the Hearts and Minds programme maybe? Or even – he let his ambition soar – go national? Or how's about one of those specials everybody seemed to be into right now?

There were other thoughts in his mind but as usual he pushed them down out of sight. Sheila Doherty would be somewhere in the hotel tonight, but he had plenty of other stuff to think about to steer his attention away from past unhappiness. No need to focus on anything right now but his career and its hopeful prospects.

Montgomery Speers, better get the name right, new Member of the Legislative Assembly, wanted to give his personal views on the peace process and how it was working out. Yeah. Wanted some publicity, more like. Anti, of course, or who'd care? But that was just how people were.

John curled his lip. He had to follow it up. It could give his career the kick start it needed.

But he didn't have to like it.

* * *

Inside the Magnifico Hotel, in the centre of newly regenerated Belfast, all was bustle and chatter, especially in the crowded space behind the catwalk. The familiar fashion show smell, a mixture of cosmetics and hair dryers, was overwhelming.

Sheila Doherty sat before her mirror, and felt a cold wave of unhappiness surge over her. How ironic it was, that title the papers gave her, today's most super supermodel. She closed her eyes and put her hands to her ears, trying to shut everything out for just one snatched moment of peace and silence.

Every now and then it came again. The pain. The despair. A face hovered before her mind's eye, the white, angry face of John Branagh, dark hair falling forward over his furious grey eyes. She deliberately blocked the thought, opening her eyes again. She needed to slip on the mask, get ready to continue on the surface of things where her life was perfect.

"Comb that curl over more to the side, will you, Chrissie?" she asked, "so it shows in front of my ear.Yeah, that's right – if you just spray it there – thanks, pet."

The hairdresser obediently fixed the curl in place. Sheila's long red-gold hair gleamed in the reflection of three mirrors positioned to show every angle. Everything had to be perfect – as perfect as her life was supposed to be. The occasion was too important to allow for mistakes.

Her fine-boned face with its clear translucent skin, like ivory, and crowned with the startling contrast of her hair, looked back at her from the mirror, green eyes shining between thick black lashes – black only because of the mascara.

She examined herself critically, considering her appearance as if it were an artefact which had to be without flaw to pass a test.

She stood up.

"Brilliant, pet," she said. "Now the dress."

The woman held out the dress for Sheila to step into, then carefully

pulled the ivory satin shape up around the slim body and zipped it at the back. The dress flowed round her, taking and emphasising her long fluid lines, her body slight and fragile as a daydream. She walked over to the door, ready to emerge onto the catwalk. She was very aware that this was the most important moment of one of the major fashion shows of her year.

Chapter 1

The lights in the body of the hall were dimmed, those focussed on the catwalk went up, and music cut loudly through the sudden silence. Francis Delmara stepped forward and began to introduce his new spring line.

For Sheila, ready now for some minutes and waiting just out of sight, the tension revealed itself as a creeping feeling along her spine. She felt suddenly cold and her stomach fluttered.

It was time and, dead on cue, she stepped lightly out onto the catwalk and stood holding the pose for a long five seconds, as instructed, before swirling forward to allow possible buyers a fuller view.

She was greeted by gasps of admiration, then a burst of applause. Ignoring the reaction, she kept her head held high, her face calm and remote, as far above human passion as some elusive, intangible figure of Celtic myth, a Sidhe, a dweller in the hollow hills, distant beyond man's possessing – just as Delmara had taught her.

This was her own individual style, the style which had earned her the nickname 'Ice Maiden' from the American journalist Harrington Smith. She moved forward along the catwalk, turned this way and that, and finally swept a low curtsey to the audience before standing there, poised and motionless.

Delmara was silent at first to allow the sight of Sheila in one of his most beautiful creations its maximum impact. Then he began to draw attention to the various details of the dress.

It was time for Sheila to withdraw. Once out of sight, she began a swift, organised change to her next outfit, while Delmara's other models were in front.

No time yet for her to relax, but the show seemed set for success.

* * *

MLA, Montgomery Speers, sitting in the first row of seats, the celebrity seats, with his latest blonde girlfriend by his side, allowed himself to feel relieved.

Francis Delmara had persuaded him to put money into Delmara Fashions and particularly into financing Delmara's supermodel, Sheila Doherty, and he was present tonight in order to see for himself if his investment was safe. He thought, even so early in the show, that it was.

He was a broad shouldered man in his early forties, medium height, medium build, red-cheeked, and running slightly to fat. There was nothing particularly striking about his appearance except for the piercing dark eyes set beneath heavy, jutting eyebrows. His impressive presence stemmed from his personality, from the aura of power and aggression which surrounded him.

A businessman first and foremost, he had flirted with political involvement for several years. He had stood successfully for election to the local council, feeling the water cautiously with one toe while he made up his mind. Would he take the plunge and throw himself whole- heartedly into politics?

The new Assembly gave him his opportunity, if he wanted to take it. More than one of the constituencies offered him the chance to stand for a seat. He was a financial power in several different towns where his computer hardware companies provided much needed jobs. He was elected to the seat of his choice with no trouble. The next move was to build up his profile, grab an important post once things got going, and progress up the hierarchy.

In an hour or so, when the Fashion Show was over, he would meet this young TV reporter for some preliminary discussion of a possible interview or of an appearance on a discussion panel. He was slightly annoyed that someone so junior had been lined up to talk to him. John Branagh, that was the name, wasn't it? Never heard of him. Should have been someone better known, at least. Still, this was only the preliminary. They would roll out the big guns for him soon enough when he was more firmly established. Meanwhile his thoughts lingered on the beautiful Sheila Doherty.

If he wanted her, he could buy her, he was sure. And more and more as he watched her, he knew that, yes, he wanted her.

* * *

A fifteen minute break, while the audience drank the free wine and ate the free canapés. Behind the scenes again, Sheila checked hair and makeup. A small mascara smear needed to be removed, a touch more blusher applied. In a few minutes she was ready but something held her back.

She stared at herself in the mirror and saw a cool, beautiful woman, the epitome of poise and grace. She knew that famous, rich, important men over two continents would give all their wealth and status to possess her, or so they said. She was an icon according to the papers. That meant, surely, something unreal, something artificial, painted or made of stone.

And what was the good? There was only one man she wanted. John Branagh. And he'd pushed her away. He believed she was a whore – a tart – someone not worth touching. What did she do to deserve that?

It wasn't fair! she told herself passionately. He went by rules that were medieval. No-one nowadays thought the odd kiss mattered that much. Oh, she was wrong. She'd hurt him, she knew she had. But if he'd given her half a chance, she'd have apologised – told him how sorry she was. Instead of that, he'd called her such names – how could she still love him after that? But she knew she did.

How did she get to this place, she wondered, the dream of romantic fiction, the dream of so many girls, a place she hated now, where men thought of her more and more as a thing, an object to be desired, not a person? When did her life go so badly wrong? She thought back to her childhood, to the skinny, ginger-haired girl she once was. Okay, she hated how she looked but otherwise, surely, she was happy. Or was that only a false memory?

"Sheila – where are you?"

The hairdresser poked her head round the door and saw Sheila with every sign of relief.

"Thank goodness! Come on, love, only got a couple of minutes! Delmara says I've to check your hair. Wants it tied back for this one."

* * *

The evening was almost at its climax. The show began with evening dress, and now it was to end with evening dress – but this time with Delmara's most beautiful and exotic lines. Sheila stood up and shook out her frock, a cloud of short ice-blue chiffon, sewn with glittering silver beads and feathers. She and Chrissie between them swept up her hair, allowing a few loose curls to hang down her back and one side of her face, fixed it swiftly into place with two combs, and clipped on more silver feathers.

She fastened on long white earrings with a pearly sheen and slipped her feet into the stiletto heeled silver shoes left ready and waiting. She moved over to the doorway for her cue. There was no time to think or to feel the usual butterflies. Chloe came off and she counted to three and went on.

There was an immediate burst of applause.

To the loud music of Snow Patrol, Sheila half floated, half danced along the catwalk, her arms raised ballerina fashion. When she had given sufficient time to allow the audience their fill of gasps and appreciation, she moved back and April and Chloe appeared in frocks with a similar effect of chiffon and feathers, but with differences in style and colour. It was Delmara's spring look for evening wear and she could tell at once that the audience loved it.

The three girls danced and circled each other, striking dramatic poses as the music died down sufficiently to allow Delmara to comment on the different features of the frocks.

With one part of her mind Sheila was aware of the audience, warm and relaxed now, full of good food and drink, their minds absorbed in beauty and fashion, ready to spend a lot of money. Dimly in the background she heard the sounds of voices shouting and feet running.

The door to the ballroom burst open.

People began to scream.

It was something Sheila had heard about for years now, the subject of local black humour, but had never before seen.

Three figures, black tights pulled over flattened faces as masks, uniformly terrifying in black leather jackets and jeans, surged into the room.

The three sub-machine guns cradled in their arms sent deafening bursts of gunfire upwards. Falling plaster dust and stifling clouds of gun smoke filled the air.

For one long second they stood just inside the entrance way, crouched over their weapons, looking round. One of them stepped forward and grabbed Montgomery Speers by the arm.

"Move it, mister!" he said. He dragged Speers forcefully to one side, the weapon poking him hard in the chest.

A second man gestured roughly with his gun in the general direction of Sheila.

"You!" he said harshly. "Yes, you with the red hair! Get over here!"

Danger Danger

Gerry McCullough

Two lives in parallel – twin sisters separated at birth, but their lives take strangely similar and dangerous roads until the final collision which hurls each of them to the edge of disaster.

Katie and her gambling boyfriend Dec find themselves threatened with peril from the people Dec has cheated.

Jo-Anne (Annie) through her boyfriend Steven finds herself in the hands of much more dangerous crooks.

Can they survive and achieve safety and happiness?

"starts with a bang and never quite lets up on the tension ... it will hook you from the beginning and keep you spell bound until the very last sentence."

Ellen Fritz, Books 4 Tomorrow

"The emotional intensity of the characters is beautifully drawn ... You care for these people."

Stacey Danson, author

an amazing, page turning, stunning novel ... equal to Belfast Girls *in every respect. I can't wait for her next novel to be published.*

***Teresa Geering**, author*

an attention-grabbing plot, strong writing, and vivid characterization, ... fast-paced and highly addictive

L. Anne Carrington, *author*

Angel in Flight:

the first Angel Murphy thriller

Gerry McCullough

Is it a bird? Is it a plane? No, it's a low-flying Angel!

You've heard of Lara Croft. You've heard of Modesty Blaise. Well, here comes Angel Murphy!

Angel, a 'feisty wee Belfast girl' on holiday in Greece, sorts out a villain who wants to make millions for his pharmaceutical company by preventing the use of a newly discovered malaria vaccine.

Angel has a broken marriage behind her and is wary of men, but perhaps her meeting with Josh Smith, who tells her he's with Interpol, may change her mind?

Fun, action, thrills, romance in a beautiful setting – so much to enjoy!

"it's a fast-paced read, ... exciting, and you can not put this book down"

Thomas Baker, *Santiago, Chile*

"I could not stop reading! ... a gripping thriller from beginning to the end"
SanMarie Lamprecht

"a fast-paced, exciting read. From the moment I read the first line, I was hooked"

Cheryl Bradshaw, *author, Wyoming, USA*

"a sassy bigger then life heroine in an action packed adventure thriller in Greece"

Book Review Buzz

Angel in Belfast:

the 2nd Angel Murphy thriller

Gerry McCullough

Angel Murphy is back, in true kick boxing form!

Alone in his cottage near a remote Irish village, Fitz, lead singer of the popular band *Raving*, hears the cries of the paparazzi outside and likens them in his own mind to wolves in a feeding frenzy.

Next morning Fitz is found unconscious, seeming unlikely to survive, and is rushed to hospital. Has he been driven to OD? Or is someone else behind this?

His friends call in Angeline Murphy, 'Angel to her friends, devil to her enemies,' to find out the truth. But it takes all Angel's courage and skills to survive the many dangers she faces and to discover the real villain and deal with him.

"brings the city and its people ... to life with evocative description and scintillating dialogue"

***Elinor Carlisle**, Berkshire, UK*

"I could not stop reading! ... a gripping thriller from beginning to the end"

SanMarie Lamprecht

"makes the troubled city of Belfast vibrant and appealing"

***P A Lanstone**, UK*

"I felt like I had been transported to Belfast's often tough, gritty streets"

***Bobbi Lerman**, USA*

"Iove the fact that we are reintroduced to characters from Belfast Girls"

***Michele Young**, UK*

"so well written that you find yourself flying through the stories"

Tom Elder

Angel in Paradise:

the 3rd Angel Murphy thriller

Angeline Murphy, 'Angel to her friends, devil to her enemies,' is on holiday in Corfu with her friend Josh Smith, hoping to relax and recharge her batteries, and perhaps develop her relationship with Josh. But Angel finds it impossible to sit back and do nothing when she learns of the assault and robbery carried out on her parents' old friend Sophie.

Before long Angel is fully involved in tracking down the brutal gang of jewel thieves who are terrorising many of the island's elderly but wealthy inhabitants. Her plan is, with Josh's help, to identify and arrest the gang's leader.

But soon Angel is in serious danger herself, from men who don't hesitate to kill to cover their tracks.

And meanwhile, the growing trust she has been feeling for Josh, as they build their relationship carefully after the disaster of Angel's first marriage, is threatened. When Angel finds Josh left for dead in an olive grove at midnight, it seems that this might be the end for them both…

Thrills, hairsbreadth escape after escape, danger, and a full helping of romance, all in the beautiful setting of Corfu, the Paradise island.

"in my opinion this is the best in this series so far."

***Tom Elder**, USA*

"it even excelled its promotion hype. One off the best I have read"

***Thea1710**, USA*

"a fast paced, brilliantly plotted and complex reading experience …

the plot twists and turns will have you on the edge of your seat"

***Soooz Burke**, Australia*

Johnny McClintock's WAR

One man's struggle against the hammer blows of life

The story of one man's struggle to maintain his faith in spite of everything life throws at him.

As the outbreak of the First World War looms closer, John Henry McClintock, a Northern Irish Protestant by upbringing, meets Rose Flanagan, a Catholic, at a gospel tent mission – and falls in love with her.

When Johnny enlists and sets off to fight in the War he finds himself surrounded by death and tragedy, which pushes his trust in God to the limit.

After more than five years absence he returns home to a bitter, war torn Ireland, where both he and Rose are seen as traitors to their own sides.

John Henry and Rose overcome all opposition and, finally, marry. But a few years later comes the hardest blow of all. Can John Henry still hang on to his faith in God?

"brilliant .. this book had me captured from the start .. moves at a fair pace throughout"
Tom Elder, *Amazon.com*

"characters you will truly care about ..

a gut-wrenching emotional ride .. a must read"

Tom Winton, author, USA

"Gerry McCullough's best book yet .. a powerful tribute to those who died for their countries and what they believed"
Juliet B Madison, author, UK

"an emotional roller coaster ride .. an epiphany .. highly recommended .. a book that will make you think about how wonderful life truly is"
Thomas Baker, Amazon.com, Santiago, Chile

"will hold you spellbound until the very last sentence .. I love this book"
Sheila Mary Belshaw, author, UK, Menorca, Cape Town

Hel's Heroes

Hel wants a hero like the ones she writes about, but does one exist?

A contemporary romance and an historic romance in one book!

Helen McFadden – Hel for short – is a successful writer of Historic Romance for the eBook market. But one day she decides that she needs to get out and experience a bit of real life. She is soon clubbing, partying and generally having a good time – and men are springing up in her life from all directions.

There's Jason, the actor, Paddy the happy-go-lucky businessman, Jordie the footballer, Markie the pop star, even Pete, her old friend.

But do any of them measure up to the heroes she writes about – especially Jack, the highwayman in her current book?

Will Hel ever learn to relate to a real man and stop expecting to meet a clone of one of her heroes?

"A fast paced, gripping tale of two romances ... and a woman's introduction to real life."

Thea, Amazon.co.uk

"What I enjoyed best ... is the author's ability to put us at Helen's side."

Barbara Silkstone, Amazon.com

"an entertaining book: a real page-turner that brings a smile to one's face"

Ronald W. Sharp, Amazon.co.uk

"an outstanding and cleverly crafted novel ... The twist at the end is awesome."

Rukia the Reader, Amazon.co.uk

Hel's Heroes 2: Christie & The Pirate

A contemporary romance and an

historic romance in one book!

Christie McCafferty's simple life as a Librarian becomes suddenly complicated when she meets Steve Armstrong. Can she trust Steve or is he a crook?

Meanwhile, Christie is reading a book called *The Pirate* by Helen – Hel for short – McFadden on her *Kindle* at night. In it, Prue is shipwrecked and picked up by a ship flying the Jolly Roger. Prue finds the pirate chief, Black Nick Hawkeye, very attractive. But surely she isn't going to fall in love with a pirate, someone she could never trust?

Christie sees that her own situation, falling for someone who may be a crook, is only too similar to Prue's with 'Hel's Hero', Nick the Pirate. How will it work out for either girl?

A pleasure to read

What a lovely addition to this series. Christie works in the library and her life is pretty smooth and easy. In fact you could say boring, nothing exciting seems to happen.

Then one day she meets Steve and suddenly her life becomes complicated. To make matters even more confusing Christie is reading a book written by Helen (Hel) McFadden about Prue who gets involved with a pirate – Black Nick Hawkeye. While in the real world Christie is trying to figure out if Steve can be trusted, at the same time in the book Christie reads how Prue is also wondering if she can let herself fall in love with Nick.

We are taken on a delightful journey as we follow both Christie and the fictional Prue. Will both find happiness or heartbreak? Have an enjoyable time finding out how it turns out for them.

Ann Stanmore, Amazon.com

Not the End of the World

A futuristic, comedy fantasy novel

Gerry McCullough

Sometime in the future, who knows how far away, all the things which people have been dreading and issuing warnings about for years are beginning to happen.

The planet earth has finally become one political unit. Its capital city is now called Nexus Luxuria. Luxury, after all, is clearly the thing most people have been aiming for all their lives.

Life has developed in an almost exactly similar fashion to the threatened forecasts. The world has at last achieved all those marvellous things we've at present only started to acquire for ourselves – global warming; over-use and exhaustion of fossil fuels; a third world with slave labour factories; globalisation of commerce until just seven multi-national companies are running the entire planet (under a titular World President with seven Vice Presidents – a Government with no real power, but considerable wealth and status); and a population kept happy by recreational drugs, which are no longer frowned on but instead encouraged. In fact, an other-earthly paradise – not!

Oh, and at a guess the future time when all this is happening is about a hundred years ahead of ours.

Or is it only fifty?

"Gerry McCullough combines a fierce and tight narrative drive with humour, imagination and lust. What more do you want?"

Malachi O'Doherty – BBC Writer in Residence, Queen's University, Belfast

"Impressive ... a furious breath-taking pace, followed by a conclusion that has you screaming: Roll on the sequel!"

Sam Millar – best-selling author of ***The Dark Place***, Belfast

Lady Molly & The Snapper

A young adult time travel adventure, set in Ireland and on the high seas

Gerry McCullough

Brother and sister Jik and Nora are bored and angry. Why does their Dad spend so much time since their mother's death drinking and ignoring them? Why must he come home at all hours and fall downstairs like a fool?

Nora goes to church and lights a candle. The cross-looking sailor saint she particularly likes seems to grow enormous and come to life. Nora is too frightened to stay.

Nora and Jik go down secretly to their father's boat, the *Lady Molly*, at Howth Marina. There they meet The Snapper, the same cross-looking saint in a sailor's cap, who takes them back in time on the yacht, *Lady Molly,* to meet Cuchulain, the legendary Irish warrior, and others.

Jik and Nora plan to use their travels to find some way of stopping their father from drinking – but it's fun, too! Or is it? When they meet the Druid priest who follows them into modern times, teams up with school bully Marty Flanagan, and threatens them, things start getting out of hand.

Meanwhile, Nora is more than interested in Sean, the boy they keep bumping into in the past ...

"the story ... flows in authentic Irish lilt and dialogue, captures the imagination"

***Book Review Buzz**, USA*

"excellent prose to suit the intended audience and has enough antics to keep any young mind turning the page"

***J.D.**, USA*

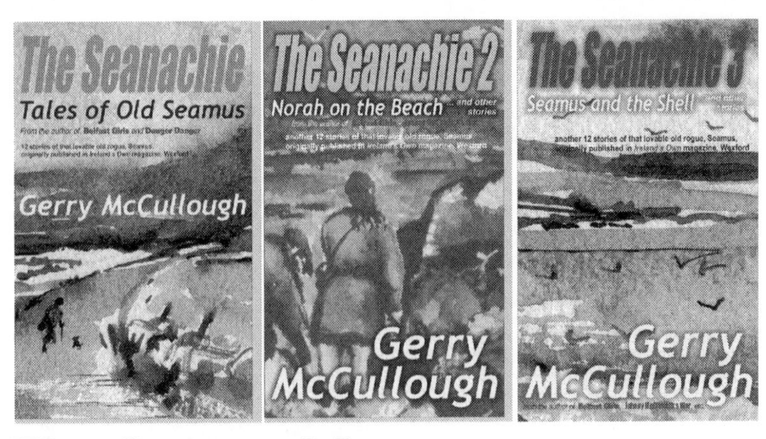

The Seanachie: *Tales of Old Seamus*

Three collections of Irish stories, set in the fictional Donegal village of Ardnakil and featuring that lovable rogue, *'Old Seamus'* – the Séanachie. All of these stories have previously been published in the popular Irish weekly magazine, *Ireland's Own*, based in Wexford, Ireland.

"heart warming tales ... beautifully told with subtle Irish humour"

Babs Morton (author)

"an irresistible old rogue, but he's the kind people love to sit and listen to for hours on end whenever the opportunity presents itself"

G. Polley (author and blogger, Sapporo, Japan)

"This magnificent storyteller has done it again. Each individual story has it's own Gaelic charm"

Teresa Geering (author, UK)

"evocative characterisation brings these stories to life in a delightful, absorbing way"

Elinor Carlisle (author, UK)

"Like the first collection ... very well written and an effortless read"

Bookworm

"so well written that you find yourself flying through the stories"

Tom Elder

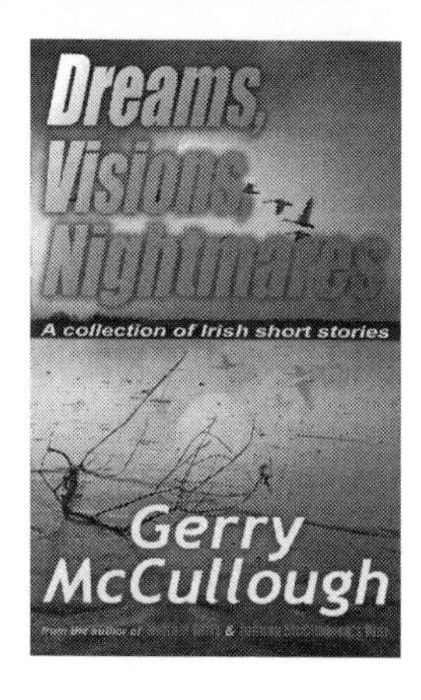

Dreams, Visions, Nightmares

A collection of eight literary and award-winning Irish short stories (newly expanded and edited)

Primroses (winner of *Cuirt international Literary Award*, Galway 2005, published in *West 47* magazine and *Cuirt Annual* 2005)

Pink Silk (published in *Verbal* magazine, Derry, 2008)

Shadows (published in *Brazen City*, Belfast 2008)

Giving Up (commended in *Seán O'Faolain Short Story Competition*, Cork 2009; published in *Sharp Sticks, Driven Nails*, Dublin 2010)

Slipping (published in *Ulla's Nib* magazine, Belfast 2009, winning Star Prize)

Ballystravey, 1988 (published by *Luciole Press*, California 2009; shortlisted for *Cuirt Award*, Galway 2010; published in *Crime after Crime* anthology, USA)

Stevie's Luck (shortlisted for the *Brian Moore Award*, Belfast, 2008)

Dark Night (Extended into full length novel, *Johnny McClintock's War* – published in 2014)

In Six Hours

... the world changed

Raymond McCullough

In just six hours the Middle East – and the world – will change forever

A friendship forged in war leads four men on separate journeys to their final destiny in a Middle East heading for meltdown

As bitter enemies race towards nuclear conflict, only a miracle can save Israel from the hostile Islamic forces surrounding her. The USA, Russia and the western world are playing with fire in the Middle East, as Iran rushes towards a nuclear climax.

While fighting the Taliban with the ISAF forces in 2012, four young men from very different backgrounds meet in Kabul, Afghanistan:

Shaul *'Solly'* Levine, an Orthodox Jew from New York City;

Micky *'Dev'* Devlin, an Irish Catholic from Boston;

Brandon *'Doubtin'* Thomas, a black Pentecostal from N. Carolina;

Khan Ali *'Zai'* Yusufzai, a Muslim Pashtun from Afghanistan.

They discover that they have more in common than they first thought and make a pact that one day they'll meet up again in Jerusalem after the prophesied Six Hour War in the Middle East, taking separate ways to a common destiny.

Meanwhile, they will keep in touch with one another as much as possible and work towards making that meeting a possibility. Will these prophecies come to pass? Will Israel itself survive the coming nuclear holocaust?

This apocalyptic thriller moves from war, to a couple of budding romances in very different locations, to more war and then the ultimate Middle East war. But even in the midst of conflict, new relationships are being formed. Action, friendship, romance ... and yet more action.

"McCullough writes with conviction and clearly knows his subject well ... [his] fluid prose draws you in and his logic and characterisation make for a believable compelling drama. Highly recommended!!!"

Juliet B Madison, author, UK

"So well written and very descriptive, you actually think you're there. Raymond has obvious knowledge of the areas he has written about as that and his passionate way of writing shine throughout. Must read book"

Tom Elder, author, USA

In One Hour

... Babylon will fall

Raymond McCullough

The debt will be called in and in one hour her destruction will come!

After a devastating, but short-lived, nuclear war, the face of the Middle East – and the whole world – has changed forever! The Ingathering – the world's greatest population transfer – has begun. Huge people groups from India and Myanmar, Pakistan and Afghanistan, from Nigeria, Zimbabwe and South Africa, and many other parts of the world, are all travelling towards one destination.

Four young men, who met first in Kabul, Afghanistan, are re-united in the heat of the logistics of this mammoth operation:

Shaul *'Solly'* Levine, an Orthodox Jew from New York City;

Micky *'Dev'* Devlin, an Irish Catholic from Boston;

Brandon *'Doubtin'* Thomas, a black Pentecostal from N. Carolina;

Aviv *'Zai'* Yusufzai, a former Muslim Pashtun from Afghanistan.

But meanwhile, not every nation is happy with the Middle East transformation. Back home in the USA, life for Brandon, Dev and their families becomes more and more difficult – and especially so for Shaul's brother, Reuben, and his family.

The world is about to change again – powerful nations are plotting another nuclear holocaust, with one man in charge. Will Shaul and his friends be able to bring out their families to safety – before Babylon falls?

"reaching out into new majestic seas ...
it takes a brave writer to take such a step. Keep going. I love it."
***Sheila Mary Taylor**, author, UK & SA*

The Whore and her Mother:

9/11, Babylon and the Return of the King

Raymond McCullough

Could the writings of the ancient Hebrew prophets be relevant to events taking place in the world today?

These Hebrew prophets – Isaiah, Jeremiah, Habbakuk and the apostle John, in *The Revelation* – wrote extensively about a latter day city and empire which would dominate, exploit and corrupt all the nations of the world. They referred to it as Babylon the Great, or Mega-Babylon, and they foretold that its fall – 'in one day' – would devastate the economies of the whole world. Have these prophecies been fulfilled already?

Is Mega-Babylon the Roman Catholic Church?
A world super-church?
Rebuilt ancient Babylon?
Brussels, Jerusalem, or somewhere entirely different?
Should this city/nation have a large Jewish population?
Why all the talk about merchants, cargoes, commodities, trade?

Can we rely on the words of these ancient prophets?
If so, what else did they foretell that is still to be fulfilled?
Do they refer to other major nations – USA, Russia, China, Europe?
What about militant Islam?

"AMAZED when I read this book ... in awe of your extensive knowledge on so many levels: Christian, Jewish, and Muslim culture; the Jewish diaspora ... Greek & Hebrew; ... thought-provoking and troublesome ... many will be offended, but you consistently build your case instead of being sensationalistic."

James Revoir, author of *Priceless Stones*

Oh What Rapture!

Is a *'Secret Rapture'* going to spare believers from the tribulation to come?

Raymond McCullough

Many are convinced that very soon an event referred to as *'The Rapture'* will take place, where bible believers all over the world will suddenly disappear, leaving society at a loss to explain this disappearance of so many. Many non-fiction books, fiction thrillers and movies have capitalised on this theme, earning a fat revenue for their authors/ producers.

But is this really what the bible teaches?
Is *'The Rapture'* genuine, or a deceptive false hope?

Are those who trust in it being duped, so that they fail to prepare themselves for what is coming?
And are they being disobedient to the clear command of the Lord?

Written by the author of *Amazon* best-selling book, *The Whore and her Mother*, also on the topic of bible prophecy, this volume focusses on the false teaching of a *'secret and separate Rapture'* – an event which is NOT supported by scripture!

This book investigates the scriptures used to back up the *'secret Rapture'* theory and clearly compares them to the other scriptures concerning the return of the Messiah, Jesus (Yeshua). The evident truth is revealed and the origins of the false *'secret Rapture'* doctrine are exposed.

Believers around the world are taught to expect persecution, sometimes even death, for their faith. More have been killed in the past century than in previous centuries combined – in China, Cambodia, Vietnam, Nigeria, Syria, Iran, Iraq, Egypt, Indonesia, etc. Yet many believers in the west confidently expect to avoid any persecution and be *'beamed up'* out of any coming tribulation!

If you thought believers were soon going to be lifted out of a worsening world situation, be prepared to meet the exciting challenge of scripture head on!

"Interesting and gave food for thought ... definitely worth a read"
Kindle customer, UK